Totally Bound Publishing books by Katherine E Hunt

Mended Hearts
Liberating Jane

Sag Harbor
The Billionaire and the Princess

I0544700

Sag Harbor

THE BILLIONAIRE AND THE PRINCESS

KATHERINE E HUNT

The Billionaire and the Princess
ISBN # 978-1-83943-965-0
©Copyright Katherine E Hunt 2021
Cover Art by Erin Dameron-Hill ©Copyright March 2021
Interior text design by Claire Siemaszkiewicz
Totally Bound Publishing

This is a work of fiction. All characters, places and events are from the author's imagination and should not be confused with fact. Any resemblance to persons, living or dead, events or places is purely coincidental.

All rights reserved. No part of this publication may be reproduced in any material form, whether by printing, photocopying, scanning or otherwise without the written permission of the publisher, Totally Bound Publishing.

Applications should be addressed in the first instance, in writing, to Totally Bound Publishing. Unauthorised or restricted acts in relation to this publication may result in civil proceedings and/or criminal prosecution.

The author and illustrator have asserted their respective rights under the Copyright Designs and Patents Acts 1988 (as amended) to be identified as the author of this book and illustrator of the artwork.

Published in 2021 by Totally Bound Publishing, United Kingdom.

No part of this book may be reproduced, scanned, or distributed in any printed or electronic form without permission. Please do not participate in or encourage piracy of copyrighted materials in violation of the authors' rights. Purchase only authorised copies.

Totally Bound Publishing is an imprint of Totally Entwined Group Limited.

If you purchased this book without a cover you should be aware that this book is stolen property. It was reported as "unsold and destroyed" to the publisher and neither the author nor the publisher has received any payment for this "stripped book".

THE
BILLIONAIRE
AND THE
PRINCESS

Dedication

To those who dream, don't give up on them.

Chapter One

Caitlyn

There is no excuse for this kind of behavior. I've promised, sworn and vowed never to fall for a bad guy again. *Take some time out*, I told myself, *learn the real Caitlyn, love yourself before you love others.* Why, oh why, then, am I half-naked in an airplane bathroom with a frickin' drunken, horny cowboy? Why indeed? He's hot, there's that, like *six-foot-two* hot. *You know what I'm talking about. The type of guy that makes you catch your breath when he brushes past you, hair a little unkempt, jaw a little too sharp.*

In my defense, I've had a very strange year and, frankly, life's gotten really, *really* complicated. Then there's the free alcohol, first time in Business Class... It's all gone to my head. I might be forgiven for getting carried away. *But still, no excuse, Caitlyn, no excuse.*

He traces a solitary finger down the outside of my thigh—my leggings hang off one ankle, dragging on the floor. My other foot, placed firmly on the closed toilet seat, is the only thing holding me up.

I lift my hair, curl it up on my head with my hands, soft lips brush against my neck. "You're so freaking hot," he slurs.

At first, I'd thought he had a Texan drawl until he'd confessed, giggling as the words came out, that he'd stolen the cowboy hat from the guy in the next seat down.

He's not Southern — he's just drunk off his head.

He brushes his fingers up my spine, circling the crux of my neck before gliding over my breasts, past the tips of my nipples, until they stop at the slick gusset of my undies. *Fuck.* For a man who smells like a brewery and has lost the capacity for coherent speech, he's pretty deft with his hands.

Pressing tightly onto my pussy, like it's the only thing holding us up, he fumbles with his trousers, pulling at his belt.

"Do you have a condom?" I ask.

"Uh…shi-it. Maybe?" He tries to grab his wallet with his one free hand and we rock back and forth as he tugs at his pocket.

Is this really happening? It was all going smoothly. Steamy, unexpected, drunken smooch in the corridor, unilateral decision to glide into the bathroom. Semi-naked foreplay.

It's all so serious, all of a sudden. Sex with a stranger. That's a sobering thought. *Is this how I want to start my new life?* It isn't part of the plan, that's for sure.

I've never done anything like this. I'm not an angel, but I've always been the *wait a few days, get to know the guy* kind of girl. Admittedly, they'd all turned out to be Mr. Emotionally Unavailable, Mr. Terrified of Commitment or Mr. Sleeps with Your Friends Plural

Behind Your Back, but hey, I'd always kept my side of the bargain.

His fumbles prove fruitless. He takes his hand off me to grab his wallet, falls backward, slams hard into the door and slides to the ground. Turns out I *was* holding him up after all.

I spin around. "You okay?" He doesn't have any visible injuries, but he's a tall man in a small space and his knees are around his ears. He still looks cute though. *God, I need to get laid.* My horny is showing.

"Oh shit!" He says it way too loud. *Fuck, he's going to get us caught.* I'm not sure what the punishment is for kinky stuff in airplane bathrooms, but I know I don't want to start my brand-new life in America in an orange jumpsuit.

"Shh," I whisper, placing my finger over my lips.

"Shh. Hee-hee." That giggle again. He's wasted–like, actually out of it. This is rapidly turning into a very bad idea, not that at any point sneaking around with a man I've just met had been a solid choice. Kissing him? That had been fun, but now it feels a little like taking advantage.

He flicks through his wallet, still sat, half on the floor, legs splayed either side of me. "Shit. I got nothing."

I lean down and put my arms around him. He nuzzles into my neck. *God, he smells delicious.* Whoever he is when he isn't half-naked and hammered, he has incredible taste in aftershave. "Let's get you up."

"Wheeee!" With one hefty yank, he's on his feet. The effort sends my back crashing against the toilet roll dispenser. It's like getting a devastatingly handsome, six-foot-two, curly haired, horny octopus to stand to attention. *Impossible.*

Stepping back to steady myself, I hear a crack. *Shit.* Hopefully, his phone isn't super important because it has just smashed into a million pieces under my foot. I kick it out of sight, sit him down on the toilet seat and pull my leggings back up. My libido is fading. Fast.

I pull up my leggings and put my top back on. "You don't wanna do it anymore?" he drawls, his face downcast.

"I don't think that's a very good idea, do you?" He can't even stand up for a start. God knows whether he can get anything else up.

"You're hot." He snakes his hands up my sweatshirt.

"Thank you. You're very, very drunk." I fasten his belt for him, inciting more giggles, and hand him his wallet, which had flown into the sink. "I think I'm going to go back to my seat. It was very nice meeting you, cowboy. Maybe we'll meet again someday in better circumstances." I might sound like I'm fobbing him off, but some part of me sort of wishes it's true. I most definitely shouldn't. The type of guy who allows himself to get in this much of a state is not boyfriend material. Not for me, anyway. But he's a sweetie, and he's cute when he giggles.

Oh, Caitlyn, you're such a damn pushover.

* * * *

The old lady in the seat next to mine looks very concerned. "Did you hear all that noise in the toilet?"

"Yes. Apparently, some drunk guy fell over."

"Oh dear." She cringes. "Some people do get carried away with the free drinks on these flights. I hope he's all right." She's been reading a guidebook on New York for the last four hours and hasn't even acknowledged my presence, but now that I've got gossip, she's all ears.

"I'm sure he's fine. So where are you flying to today?"

She closes her book and looks at me. "New York." Her eyes widen with excitement. Bless her. She has to be at the very least in her seventies. I see a little of myself in her, always excited by new experiences, no matter how old I get. That's the only way to live.

"Well, yes. I meant for business or pleasure."

"I'm going to see my son. He's got a fancy job in Manhattan, going to show me the sights." She curls her lips into the biggest grin.

"Oh, that's lovely."

Something loud crashes behind us. "Oh dear," she mutters. "What now?"

A flash of white comes racing past our seats. A butt. A very naked butt attached to a very handsome, drunken, giggly cowboy.

"Shit," I whisper under my breath. Maybe I shouldn't have left him to his own devices after all. He turns and waves his not-insignificant appendage at a room full of dozing passengers before a hand reaches through the curtain behind him and pulls his drunken, naked butt into First Class.

"Good lord," she says, raising an eyebrow. "I haven't seen one like that since my Henry was alive."

I turn to her and smile, hiding my deep regret at my rash decision not to get cowboy's number before I'd left him. "Lucky you," I reply.

Chapter Two

Caitlyn

I swear, my heart skips a beat when the car pulls up in front of my new home. The sun is still shining down on this late June afternoon, reflecting off the ocean, and I refuse to let the fact that I haven't slept for twenty-four hours let me enjoy this moment any less.

I pause for a second to take in my bearings as the driver opens the door for me. He leads me up through a small front garden to a beautiful brick-built house. Hanging baskets and potted plants adorn the wooden front porch, on which I imagine at some point people have sat on rocking chairs and looked out at the sea behind me, waiting for a boat to bring their loved ones home. Orange and pink begonias fill the air with a light perfume and entice a couple of buzzing bees. A large, white, wooden sign swings silently over the front door on its black wrought-iron fittings.

This will be my home and place of work for the next year. A fresh start. The life I want and not the life that has been chosen for me.

Turning to face the sea, I breathe in the familiar salty air. Boats clank and chime, moored along the bay only a hundred yards away. My phone in my hand, I immortalize this moment with a picture.

My heart is beating so fast that I can hardly breathe. This is so exciting.

Born in an Irish coastal town, the smell of the sea, the seagulls' cry, it's second nature to me. Saltwater runs through my veins. Of course, I can't compare this town and mine. No sticks of rock and arcades here. I'd only seen a few streets as we drove through the town to get here, but I can smell the exclusivity in the air. This is not a working-class seaside town, this place is elegant, clean, invested in.

The door opens, and a woman, about my age, welcomes me into my new abode. Long, dark straight hair and olive skin, she is strikingly beautiful. She flashes a perfect smile and opens up her arms. "Caitlyn? Hi, I'm Jen."

"Hi." No chance of getting past without a hug, I reluctantly oblige. American culture is already coming at me with two tight arms and a squeeze. She smells like freshly washed linen and vanilla, reminding me that I haven't washed in a day. A quick spritz of deodorant at the airport might have been a good idea, especially if I'd known there were going to be hugs.

"Welcome to Sag Harbor. Come in, come in." She ushers me into the house and thanks the driver, who places my two sad-looking suitcases inside the door. My whole, entire life is in those cases and they're so battered that it's a wonder they survived the voyage. The journeys they've accompanied me on, the memories they hold… These are no ordinary suitcases. Ah, there'll be time to get them repaired. I'm planning on staying a while.

The driver hands me my guitar and I sling it over my shoulder then leaves, as silently as he arrived, as if he were never here to begin with.

"Do we… Should I have tipped him? I'm not sure how it works and I read that I'm supposed to tip everybody." My mum would have tipped the milkman if she could. She was always getting out her purse to thank somebody for their good work. '*They need it more than us*,' she would say, even though quite often the opposite was the case. I like to think I inherited that quality from her, despite my grandmother trying to teach me otherwise. Ironic really, as she could afford it.

"No, it's fine, he works for us." Jen smiles in that slightly condescending way people do when explaining something to someone who should really know that by now. She looks at my guitar. I can see her mind whirring. I don't look or dress very much like the qualifications on my CV. I've interned in some of the most prestigious newspapers in the UK, assisted some very important people and yet here I am, wild curly blonde hair that cannot be tamed, sweatpants and my old faithful guitar on my shoulder.

I smile reassuringly. It tends to put people at ease. I have the kind of face that relaxes people, makes them feel at home, or so I've been told.

"Ah, okay." He works for *us*. *Who is 'us'? My new employer, The Baresi Corporation?* Books with a capital B, that's what they're most known for now. The website that makes other online booksellers quiver in fear. They also own some of the biggest TV channels in the States and around the world, and probably every newspaper and magazine everyone was reading on the plane over. But digital media is what everybody wants now.

Journalism, a dying art, or so everybody insists on telling me. But here I am, proving them all wrong.

"So, come on through. This is where you'll be working and I'll take you on up to your apartment." She's wearing the most beautiful fitted blue dress, which stops just below her knees, and nude heels that look like they cost more than my flight over. I regret, somewhat, my decision to have gone with the sweatshirt and messy bun combo that I save for traveling and binge-watching. I look down and pick Pringles crumbs off of my boob. Not the most auspicious start.

The inside of the building is as gorgeous as the outside, with exposed brick walls and original features. Two desks, fully supplied with laptops and printers, create an office space. Comfy chairs sit in the library corner, surrounded by bookshelves filled with leather-bound antique books, and a small kitchen with a rather expensive-looking coffee maker finishes the room.

There's a strong chance I'll be spending my evenings poring over those books, my own collection having been shared amongst my friends at home. I miss all of them already, the books, not the friends, although I miss them too, just less. Only a couple of well-thumbed favorites sit at the bottom of my case, waiting to adorn the shelves of my new apartment.

"Has anybody gone into detail with you yet about what you'll be doing?" I follow Jen up a tight, spiral metal staircase and imagine myself having to lug my two suitcases up here. I'll save that for tomorrow morning.

"Yes and no. Magazine start-up. I understand that I won't be dealing with either the financial or advertising side of things, just reporting on events and writing articles about local businesses and products."

"Perfect. That's exactly it. Just the reporting side of things, we'll do literally everything else."

There's that turn of phrase again. *We, us,* why not 'they'? Is she the spokesperson for the entire company?

At the top of the stairs, a small entry hall leads to a beautiful open-plan apartment, in much the same style as the office below. Restored antique furniture mingles with modern appliances. Someone has extremely good taste.

"When do my colleagues start?"

"Ha, ha! Oh, you're not joking." The perfect grin on her face freezes, like a rebooting robot, as she composes herself. "Yeah, no, there's only two of you on this team and uh, let's just say that your boss isn't exactly known for his great work ethic." *Fantastic.*

"So I'm basically on my own?"

"Not at all. The Baresi Corporation is here for you. We can supply you with anything you need, material or otherwise. Think of it as being head of a very small department of one." She laughs, drily, at her own joke. It sounds like I've been completely fucked over from where I'm standing.

"So have you worked for the Baresi family long then?"

She gives me another flash of that perfectly practiced smile. "Since birth. I'm Ginevra Baresi."

Ginevra Baresi? Presenter of *The Morning Show*. The Morning Show. She's a big deal over here. Live from The Gutzwiller House in New York, celebrity guests, big names. She's a household name over here and only thirty years old at that.

Well, fuck me sideways.

"You," I reply, unable to formulate a coherent sentence. Jen is the big boss's daughter, the only daughter out of six children. Well, I say children. Obviously they're all grown adults, living in the shadow of their father, Guillermo Baresi, the most powerful media mogul in the world. And my new boss. Well, my boss's boss's boss.

"Me." She cracks a genuine smile this time. "Sorry. I should have said something sooner."

Shit, now I'm just making it awkward. "No, that's fine. You're probably used to people knowing who you are. I have no excuse, except that I just changed time zones and I haven't slept in a day." I'm blathering on, but this is so embarrassing. I should have recognized her immediately. *Great one, Caitlyn, you're only half an hour in and you've already made your first blooper.* Normally it takes me at least a day before my unfiltered mouth insults or embarrasses myself or others around me.

"Oh my God, I am so sorry, you must be exhausted. Look, there's food in the fridge and your bed is all made up." I might have to forego food. That king-size bed is calling my name.

"That's so kind. Really, you've been great."

"I'm afraid you've been thrown in the deep end with this. My, uh, *your* boss should have been here to welcome you and set all of this up. I'm just filling in for him, really, this isn't my field at all." The way she keeps spitting out the word *boss*, as if she hates the man, makes me very uneasy. "Here's my card. Give me a call tomorrow when you're feeling more human and I'll show you around."

I follow her down to lock up for the night. Walking back through the office, I brush my hand along the perfect wood grain of my new desk. *Caitlyn Walsh, Editor.* The nameplate says it all.

Caitlyn, you've arrived, you've done it. Four years of back-breaking studying and unpaid internships was absolutely worth it to see my name on that desk. *Chief of myself, that's my unofficial title, but nobody has to know that, right?* When this thing is up and running, I'll have a whole host of employees, anyway.

Editor. The dream.

Chapter Three

Caitlyn

Mornings are not my favorite part of the day. Especially when morning, where I am, is late afternoon in yesterday's time. The sound of birdsong resonates around the loft, loudly announcing that it is indeed time to get up, but my eyes strongly oppose any attempt at opening them. They remain on UK time and they are not having any of my nonsense.

Only a good cup of tea can bring me out of my fog. Strong tea. I've brought a box of Yorkshire's finest teabags, neatly packed in my suitcase, but that still sits downstairs. Maybe my hosts have thought to stock up for their English guest.

I stumble over to the kitchen. After a quick shower last night I'd thrown on my favorite Muppets T-shirt, stashed in my backpack for emergencies, and a pair of undies I'd put in for the same reason then sank under the covers. There had been absolutely zero inclination to unpack.

"Holy fuck!"

I slam my foot into a butt sticking out from under the sink. A not unattractive butt. Firm and well-proportioned. It is wearing jeans with a hint of tight, white boxer shorts, the brand name of which is displayed along the elastic for everyone to see. Well, when I say 'everyone', that's going on the assumption that it's only me and the butt in the loft right now, and even then, that's one too many.

"Ow!" The butt, either reacting to my foot having given it a good shove or hearing my less than ladylike cry, veers toward me before revealing the rest of the body attached to it.

"Fu-uck." This time the word slips out more quietly as my brain takes in the situation. *Him. From the plane.* I'd recognize that body anywhere, and, let's be honest, I've seen most of it, close up.

The ten-gallon hat having presumably been given back to its owner, a head full of wild, dark curls are revealed, in all their glory. He's neither rootin' nor tootin' like he was in that bathroom yesterday, but fuck it if it isn't my cowboy.

"Morning," he says, rubbing his butt and grinning at me, not in the slightest bit bothered by the fact that I've just found him hiding under the sink in my kitchen. American stalkers are brazen. I didn't realize I'd be needing a bodyguard on the first day. He's also not wearing a T-shirt and those abs are scrambling my brain.

"Cowboy." My mouth, entirely independent from the rest of my body, decides to throw me under the bus.

"What?" He looks at me blankly.

"Nothing." I grab the first thing that comes to hand to protect myself and end up brandishing a wooden spatula at him. *Dangerous.* "Um, what are you doing in my kitchen? And why are you half naked?"

The man is a god. Perfectly formed. A person cannot possibly be expected to concentrate on their tea and toast when faced with that body. A flush rises in my chest and my nipples do, well, what nipples do encountering such splendor. I put one arm tightly across my chest.

My body wants to have an urgent conversation about this guy, but I'm not listening. My brain is assessing the situation, especially as I had never expected to see the stranger from the plane again. Has he tracked me down? Stolen my address from my wallet? No, nothing I own has this address on it, only my phone, and I definitely had that on me when I arrived.

I take a step back. *Has he come back to finish the job? Congratulations, Caitlyn, you've lived in America less than one day and you've already managed to insult the boss's daughter and find yourself a handsome, sexy stalker.* None of this was in the job description.

"No, not the spatula." He chuckles and puts up his hands. "My bad. I didn't know you'd moved in yet. I was just checking the plumbing under the sink." He holds out a dusty hand. "Enrico Baresi, everyone calls me Hank."

Baresi. *Another one? They're everywhere.* He doesn't recognize me. Thank God for beer goggles. The state he was in yesterday, it's not surprising he has no memory of me.

Say something, woman. "Well, hi, Hank Baresi, I'm Caitlyn Walsh. Nice to meet you." We're still shaking hands, and my deadly weapon is still being waved at him. I lower the spatula and take back my hand. He grins. Trust has been instilled.

"Yeah. I'm renovating a house up the road. Just got back from a trip to Europe with my brother yesterday, I didn't know you'd moved in yet. Sorry. I, uh, needed to check the sink to see how I'd done the plumbing." He grabs his T-shirt and slips it on, covering up those delicious abs. *To be fair, I'm definitely staring at them.*

"Oh, you're a builder then?" How do they say it in American? "Construction. You work in the construction business, do you?" The words are coming out but nothing is processing. I've seen this man's dick. His big, *big* dick. Kind of felt it too, rubbing up against my back. My lady parts do a jump for joy at the memory and I slam my hand onto the counter to hold on for dear life.

"Oh no, that's just a hobby. I'm your new boss — well more of a colleague to be exact. This place is mine. I bought it and renovated it. *The End*, the magazine, it's all my idea. Well, my father's idea, but I'm running it."

Fuck, Caitlyn. You nearly banged your boss.

Of course, karma isn't going to thank me for walking away instead of taking advantage of this man in his inebriated state. Yesterday his dick had danced around in front of me and he'd fondled my clit in a public bathroom and today I find myself standing in front of him in a fucking Muppets T-shirt, boobs unleashed, hair resembling Big Bird's butt.

Perfect.

"I am so excited about it. This is an amazing opportunity, honestly, my dream job."

His eyes crinkle up at the sides and my vagina melts into a puddle of warm desire. "Well, I'm glad to hear that. Look... I've really got to get back to work, I was just wondering, why did you call me 'cowboy'?"

"I...uh..." *Make something up. Anything. Lie.* "I was on the same flight as you yesterday." *You idiot.*

Hank's face turns puce, right back to his ears. "Ah."

Why didn't you just lie? He clearly has no memory of you and the way he held your clitoris and grazed his lips along the back of your neck. Stop thinking about it. Stop it.

"Yeah." His eyes glaze over. His brain surely taking a moment to process the fact that I've seen his cock in all its glory. I've even fondled it somewhat, over his trousers, while he was sticking his tongue down my throat, although that part seems to elude him.

"Cool, cool. Well, I've got to get going." He steps away, can't leave fast enough. "Jen tells me she's showing you around this afternoon. We won't start work on the magazine until Monday, so you know, take a few days to get acquainted with the place. Did she tell you about the car? The Audi out the front, the black one? That's yours to use as you see fit. Insured, everything." He backs away as he is speaking, the words spurting out one after the other without pausing for breath.

"Oh, okay, thanks. Uh, see you Monday."

"Yeah, great meeting you, Caitlyn." He does finger guns and looks like he instantly regrets it, putting them awkwardly back into their holsters without even blowing on them. "Looking forward to working together."

"With all of our clothes on," I reply, trying to break the awkwardness with a bit of humor. *I should stop talking now.*

He frowns for a second, then flashes another grin at me. "Fully dressed, got it. Bye, Caitlyn."

He leaves the apartment so fast that he practically flies down the stairway like a fireman on a pole, can't get away from me quick enough.

Chapter Four

Hank

Enzo always knows what to do. He's been solving my problems ever since I peed my pants in first grade.

I throw myself down on the plush sofa in his waiting room. "Is he in?"

"He's on a call, Hank." Evelyn has her orders. It isn't done to just barge in and bother the CEO, but this is *me*.

I push out my bottom lip and quiver it a bit. "You sure?"

"Don't you give me those puppy-dog eyes, Enrico Baresi." She buzzes me through. Nobody can resist my charm, not even Evelyn, and she's as hard as nails.

"What's up, fuckwit?" says Enzo. Being the youngest child has certain advantages but four older brothers isn't one of them. It was decided very early on that Fuckwit was my name and they've never faltered.

I go to take a deep breath, center myself, but it comes out as more of a resigned sigh. "I have a little situation."

"It's called a dick. You have a little dick."

"Hilarious. I can see why they made you CEO."

"They made me CEO because I'm the only Baresi son who never complains about *little* situations. I fix them."

"It's Leo's fault. He gave me a sleeping pill on the plane yesterday — "

"Wait! Let me just stop you right there. You accepted pills from Leo?" He lifts his head and stares at me in desperation. "Our brother, Leo." I look down at my feet, avoiding his icy glare. He has a point. Leo isn't exactly known for being sober, or reliable, or trustworthy in any way. Enzo's right. He's always right. Why the hell *had* I done that?

"Yes, Leo. I know it was dumb. Anyway, so then, for laughs, he spikes my drink."

He shuffles the papers on his desk, pushes his reading glasses back up his nose and stares down them at me. "I don't know if I want to hear the rest of this story."

"You don't, but I shall continue. From what I've been told, I stole a cowboy hat and locked myself in a toilet. There may have been public nudity." Okay, there was definitely public nudity, but confessing that would involve Enzo shouting at me and my head is pounding right now.

"May? For fuck's sake, Hank. Tell me you didn't have sex with anybody? Did you use protection? Did anybody film it?"

"I don't think so. I think I remember a woman in the bathroom with me." *Fuck.* There *was* a woman. A hot, sexy, blonde woman. *Or maybe she was a brunette.* She had tits, I remember that. "Yeah, there was definitely a woman. I don't think we fucked though."

A retching sound emanates from Enzo's throat. He grabs his bottle of water. "You don't *think* you fucked anybody. Great. So why exactly are you here?"

"That's not the problem." And here we are at the crux of the issue, the real reason for my visit. My chest tightens. Why can I not even breathe around this man? He's the good brother, the one who used to pull my other brothers off me. We're grown men now, but just being in his presence stresses me out.

"*That's* not the problem? What? Was this a prelude to you having a public orgy on live TV?"

As if I'd do that, in a country where my dad owns seventy-five percent of the media. Give me some credit. "No. you know that hotshot British journalist you hired to work on my magazine?"

"Yes. You didn't sleep with *her*, did you? Papa's going to be pissed."

"No, God no. Not that I wouldn't, she's cute." I don't have much to go on, just a literal kick up the butt and a five-minute conversation, but I wouldn't say no to getting to know her better. "No, I mean she saw everything. She was on the plane."

"You want me to fire her because she saw your cock at half-mast?" My eyes drop to my much-maligned cock. *Don't listen to him, big guy. You do your best.*

"No. I wanted to know what to do about it."

"Does she know you know she saw your wilted cock?" I sink my hand instinctively to my crotch. His jibes hurt. My dick shrinks into itself, just like it did growing up when my brothers all decided they were going to use my crotch for batting practice.

"She brought it up, called me 'cowboy', like it hadn't even fazed her.

"I like this woman already. Listen, fuckwit, you're going to just have to get over it. This is your absolute final chance with Papa, and you only got it because, for some unknown reason, you're Mama's favorite little guy. So suck it up and go to work. Now get. I have real grown-up work to do. And go get your mild-mannered cock tested for all the things."

There's no denying that Enzo made a good argument. Caitlyn was quite blasé about what she'd seen. And our relationship is purely business. This doesn't have to be a problem. It's fine, we'll be fine. So she's seen my cock. It's probably all over the internet by now, anyway. Just like the last time.

I picture her in that oversized T-shirt she'd been wearing this morning and the way she'd looked at me when I stood up. My gut does a little roll. Those wild, frizzy curls and that accent.

No. We'll keep things purely professional and it'll stay that way. I don't need to rock the boat right now. I need the magazine because I need my allowance. Replacement flooring, especially the good stuff, doesn't pay for itself.

I head back down to my truck and my phone rings — *La Cucaracha.* "Yes, Ted."

"Hank, it's Ted." *Hi, Ted.* "Are you back from Europe?"

"Yup."

"Great, I need a hand this afternoon and you're the only person who can help."

Half an hour later, I'm standing on his doorstep, toolbox in hand, waiting for my orders.

"What do you need fixing?"

"Why do you assume I need something fixing?" There's no need to reply, I know what my friends want when they ask me for *a hand*. "Okay, well, it's not anything that needs fixing, exactly. I need your help assembling some furniture. Turns out I don't own a screwdriver or understand instructions."

Ted and Claire are probably the only ones out of our little gang of friends who have already turned into grownups. Proper jobs, well for Ted anyway, a junior partner in his father's law firm, marriage and now a baby on the way. Their house is much like the ones we all grew up in, except with fewer bedrooms. They're the only ones with a full-time staff too. It's like the guy who used to get drunk and jerk around with me is now morphing into his dad.

He takes me up to the nursery. Identical pieces of wood are strewn around the room. "Did you…did you take *everything* out of the box?" *Why would he do that? Why?*

"Claire said I have to put together the crib and something called a changing station, so that I bond with the baby and acknowledge that I'm going to be a father. I love my wife—don't get me wrong, she's my everything—but she looks like the size of a house and I haven't slept in two weeks because of the snoring. It's like an allergic elephant and she is mean, Hank, real mean. But sure, building furniture is going to make me feel like a dad."

Obviously fatherhood wasn't going swimmingly for Ted. I thank my lucky stars that I didn't do anything stupid in that airplane bathroom last night. Instinctively, I grab hold of my wallet. Why then, if I'm so sure of my innocence, do I have a sinking feeling I'd been checking for condoms in it?

"Give me the instructions. I'm assuming I have to get this done quietly and without telling anybody." I wink at him. My friends and I have spent our lives getting each other out of trouble, especially when it came to girlfriends.

The four musketeers. Ted, Jonny, Chad and me. The rich kids in a world where nobody has less than at least a few million in the bank, except me. Apart from my allowance, my inheritance is gone. I'm a billionaire by association.

He nods nervously and rubs his hands together. "She must never know, Hank. She must never know."

After a good hour of assemblage and a few extra nuts and bolts from my stock to secure everything tightly, we had a nursery all set up and ready to welcome Ted and Claire's baby. We decide to celebrate with a beer on the terrace. Well, it's only fair I should receive some compensation.

"So have you met your new editor-in-chief yet?"

"Oh yeah, we've met." Ted loves a good story, especially one involving me being high and naked.

He's not disappointed by my tale of drunken hijinks, ten thousand feet up. "Leo's a dick."

"Yup." My second oldest brother is a drunk and a womanizer, on his third wife and probably already sleeping with the fourth. He is also second-in-command, after Enzo, both in and out of the job. Not counting my father, of course, the supreme leader of everyone.

"So what's she like, this Caitlyn?" He raises his eyebrows.

Does he want her credentials or her bra size? "You mean, is she hot?"

"No." He laughs nervously. "Yes, of course I do. I'm a married man now. I have to live vicariously through my single friends and their disastrous love lives."

"Yeah, maybe. She's a colleague. You know I don't want to think of her like that." If I say it enough times, to enough people, it will be true. As long as she never stares at my body like she was doing this morning or calls me 'cowboy' with that accent again.

"You. Hank Baresi. The man who famously once announced that he only dated models doesn't want to objectify women?"

"She comes highly recommended, top of her class at college. Degree in journalism, master's in photography. I need her on my side. I'm not going to fuck it up by sleeping with her."

"Plus, she's already seen your dick."

"What's that supposed to mean?" Why has everyone got in in for my dick today?

"The number of women you've slept with, it's probably worn down and covered in pustules."

I'm pretty sure that's not how that works. *You can't wear down a penis. Can you?*

"I haven't slept with *that* many women."

"Hank, you know that Jason Derulo song about women in every country? That's you, man. He wrote that song about you."

Ted's obviously jealous. He's only ever known Claire, in the biblical sense. I choose not to rise to any more remarks about my cock or my sex-life today. "I'm well-traveled."

"Okay, if that's what you kids are calling it these days."

I have changed, for the better. There'd been a time in my life when spending my inheritance and having a good time was more important than settling down, getting a job, like Ted here. But with age has come wisdom, or so I like to think. No more running away, I fully intend to make a go of my house flipping business, work in media to get my parents off my back and maybe invest in my love life more too.

Okay, I'd *maybe* fucked some woman in an airplane bathroom yesterday. Shit happens when you travel with Leo. It doesn't mean if the right person comes along that I won't be ready for a more permanent situation. I'm settling down, opening myself up to new possibilities.

And none of this, absolutely none of this, involves Caitlyn.

We need to set boundaries if my business plan is going to work and I am ready and willing to be the man to do it. Shouldn't be hard to do anyway. There's no way any woman would be interested in me after seeing me high and naked on that plane.

Chapter Five

Caitlyn

A cup of tea in my hand, stuff unpacked, I sit back on my very comfortable couch in my luxury loft apartment and mull over the news that my airplane hook-up and my new boss are one and the same person.

Any fantasies I'm planning to have — while alone with my shower head — are not to involve the naked cowboy from the plane.

That's going to be a tough one. The trace of his lips on my body, his fingers sliding down onto my pussy, just the memory of it makes me quiver. And that kiss, the way he whisked me up into his arms like Johnny did to Baby.

I put down my mug and call Jen to see if she wants to hang out. I can't possibly sit around here all day fantasizing about my boss's aptitude for fingering.

Luckily she's still up for a visit of Sag Harbor, so I shower and do something with my hair. I'm not one for heavy makeup, on my days off but I suspect that this town has more than its fair share of beautiful people and I don't want Jen to be embarrassed to be in my presence.

I have to stop wishing that the first time I'd met sober Hank Baresi I'd not been half-dressed with old-crone hair. It weighs on me. Looking a bit more polished would have been preferential, but the choice hadn't really been mine. Who comes into someone's home and climbs under their sink without at least knocking?

My mind keeps replaying the fact that I'd stared at his abs and he'd seen me stare at his abs. Back in England, there's a strict hierarchy, I know my place. Here, however, things are different. I had been so looking forward to finally being judged for my talent as a writer, for the years of hard work I'd poured into my education and for simply being me, but it's only been twenty-four hours and I've got a terrible sinking feeling that I'm already mucking everything up.

The incident this morning and the one on the plane, both of them could set back my dreams of being a successful journalist. Opportunities like this don't come along every day and I need to grasp this one by the horns and never let go. Any intentions toward Hank could seriously jeopardize that. I'm not willing to take that chance.

* * * *

Jen picks me up outside in a sporty little two-seater that looks like it should be driven by a middle-aged man with a small penis. "Hope you don't mind company for lunch. I forgot that I was meeting up with friends. One of my besties, Claire, is due any day now, and we wanted to have some girl time before she gives birth." I'm still jet-lagged and I hardly even know Jen. It's hard not to be nervous. I need to start making a good impression.

"Oh, I hope I'm not intruding."

"Not at all. I couldn't leave you alone when you don't know anybody. That's not how we do things around here." That warms my heart. There's something very genuine about Jen. No airs and graces about her, when she has every right to act entitled if my internet searches this morning were anything to go by. She's good people.

"You've been so kind and welcoming."

"I feel bad that you're basically going to be working on your own this year and it's all Hank's fault."

"I think he's going to be involved. I met him this morning. He said he'd be there on Monday." The image of his abs flashes into my mind, which in turn reminds me of his dick, and I can't help but blush. Can she tell what's going through my mind right now? I bloody hope not, for her sake.

"My little brother is going to get up early on a Monday to go to work? That boy hasn't done a decent day's work in his life. He dropped out of college, quit every job my dad gave him and left on a plane, only to come back three years later."

"Oh, okay." *It just gets better and better.* "So why is he setting up a magazine?"

"They're cutting him off."

"What are they cutting off?" That sounds rather drastic. Hopefully not that majestic cock.

"His allowance. If he doesn't work for them, he doesn't get any money. They're fed up with him and his house flipping and his lack of interest in the family business." *No pressure on me to make this magazine a success, then. Great.* I let out a loud harrumph, and she laughs at my disgruntled reaction. "Yeah, that's why I'm taking you out. Cocktails, my treat."

Becky and Claire are lounging outside, soaking up the late spring sun. The short one with the spiky hair looks like she's due to pop any minute, her belly's bigger than Luxembourg. She has to be Claire.

Becky, however, is quite the opposite. Easily a foot taller than all of us, her skinny legs making up seventy-five percent of her body. Her long, blonde wavy hair and pale skin would be similar to mine if I spent three days in the hair salon with my head in a bowl of keratin and with a face mask on. As I pull up a chair next to her, it occurs to me that to everyone around us we must look like those edited before-and-after photos that pop up on social media, except that this woman is permanently photoshopped to perfection.

"Hi, I'm Claire. I ate all the pies."

She moves to get up and hug me. "Don't get up. We'll do a British hello." I wave like the queen and it brings a smile to her tired face.

"And I'm Rebecca Sinclair." A limp hand is waved in my face in such a regal way, I can't figure out if I'm supposed to shake or kiss it. I go for the shake and I just end up lifting and lowering her fingers for half a minute until she pulls her hand away. "And you are?"

The assurance in her voice, the lack of eye contact. Does she have any idea how intimidating she is? That is most likely the point of her behavior. Assume superiority right from the get-go, and let me know where I stand. She's very good at it.

"Caitlyn." She squints at me, waiting for more. "Walsh, Caitlyn Walsh." I can see the cogs whirling around in her mind. Should she know who I am, and am I in any way important or useful to her?

"She's Hank's editor," says Jen.

Becky lets out a snort. "Oh Jesus, I hope you bought a return ticket."

Jen coughs, and Claire looks away in embarrassment. Not a single person has any faith that Hank and I are going to pull this off, do they? I haven't worked so damned hard to get my degree and traveled thousands of miles to be disrespected like this. I'll show them, if I have to run the whole magazine myself, which, if what I am led to believe is true, is not out of the realm of possibility.

We order drinks. "So tell us about you, Caitlyn," says Claire, rubbing her stomach.

"What's there to tell? Grew up in London. My mother passed away when I was thirteen, I lived with my grandmother until I was sixteen and then I took a secretarial apprenticeship. Worked my way up the ladder until I was running a small start-up. Jacked it all in for university and here I am four years later."

I'm waiting for one of them to proclaim, 'How quaint'? It's evident I'm among money here. None of these women get out of bed for anything less than a million, and that's just their allowances.

"You've come far." Jen has begun to grow on me. Her sincerity is genuine, unlike Becky with the nice hair who defined me as a minion the minute she has laid eyes on me.

"I hear you've met Hank already," says Claire. Becky glances over at her and smirks as if they know a naughty secret. How could they possibly know about me and Hank? Has he remembered, has someone told on us? "On the plane." They *know*.

My heartbeat rises. I panic. I can't let them see that they're affecting me in this way. *Breathe.* Say something, anything, just say it calmly.

"What do you say in America? I plead the fifth. Is that it?" This gets a giggle out of Becky. Am I rising in her esteem? Surely not.

Jen leans in. "What are you talking about?"

"Your brother was waving his cock around…again."

My relief that they were only talking about Hank and not 'me and Hank' is quickly replaced by the realization that I'm dealing with a serial stripper.

"Again?" I spit it out, trying to hide my disappointment at my new colleague's penchant for nudity. "This isn't something I need to worry about in the office, is it? Because that's not really how we do things in the UK."

"As far as I know, he's only done it twice before. There was that one time in Chad's Jacuzzi but that was just because he thought there was nobody home," replies Becky.

"So that makes four in total," says Claire, holding up four fingers for us all to see. *All right, I can count.*

My dream job begins to crumble before my very eyes. Maybe I can just tell Hank that he doesn't have to come to work, that I'll cover for him? A high-society magazine run by somebody who is rapidly gaining notoriety for his naked shenanigans. They certainly do things differently on this side of the pond.

Jen pales. "Jesus Christ, if it's not one thing it's another." It must be such shit having to deal with a brother like Hank. She works hard, she lives a respectful life and her drunken, pill-popping brother shames her at every opportunity. I can see why their parents are cutting him off.

Claire has the decency to blush. "Sorry. Ted told me. I shouldn't have said anything."

You shouldn't have teased Hank's sister about his naked shenanigans? Yeah, probably. Becky on the other hand adores seeing Jen squirm. The delight in her eyes, as she swirls the straw around her drink and chuckles to herself leaves a sour taste in my mouth.

"So when are you due?" I ask Claire.

"Another month, if you can believe it, but I'm ready to go if he wants to come out early."

"You keep that guy in there until he's fully baked," says Becky. "He needs to do as much growing as he can while he's still in there, if he's going to beat genetics."

Claire doesn't reply. She lowers her eyes, pinches her lips and takes a deep, nasal breath. She's a petite woman, small and perfectly formed. *Is her height a common teasing point too?* I'm assuming, now, that her husband isn't a tall man.

This 'besties' lunch is fraying at the edges. When Jen mentioned that we were meeting up with her friends, I thought my presence would be an issue. It hadn't even occurred to me that they already didn't get along.

Small talk fills the time while we wait for our food. Claire fills us baby novices in on the last-minute preparations for the arrival of her son. Her husband is the first son of the first son and so their child will be the first son of the first son too. I'm not up on my American aristocracy, as it were, but I do know a thing or two about royalty and I get that this is a pretty big deal.

"And of course, the baby shower's tomorrow. Ted's mother hasn't spared a dime. She hired this guy who normally does weddings. I'm not privy to everything, but we had a cake tasting a couple of weeks ago. We couldn't decide because they were all so delicious, and we got so many in the end." I look at the half-eaten salads abandoned on the tables surrounding ours. A niggling feeling tells me people here don't eat that much dessert. There's going to be an awful lot of leftover cake.

"Caitlyn should come," says Jen, smiling at me.

"Oh, I don't think—" I hardly know them. That wouldn't be appropriate at all.

"For the magazine," adds Jen, quickly, before I say something I'll regret. "You don't get more high Hamptons society than Ted's family." Jen grabs my arm. "They're positively presidential. Or at least his great-grandfather was."

For the magazine. Of course. Why would she be inviting you to prestigious parties Caitlyn? Know your place, woman. "Oh I'd love to."

"Do you have a photographer?" asks Becky, in a rare moment of giving a shit.

"That would be me. Master's in photojournalism. I'm my own one-man—well, one-woman—show." I do jazz hands as I'm saying it and laugh at my own joke while Becky remains stoic in front of me.

"How quaint," she replies. Ah, there it is. Clichéd rich person statement, I've been expecting you.

The waiter brings over our food and we eat in relative silence. Tensions are high among these women. They are all lost in their own private thoughts. A few glasses of rosé and several uneaten salads later and the atmosphere has become a touch more convivial.

We say our goodbyes to Becky and Claire, who are going to their weekly mani-pedi appointments, and Jen invites me for a digestive stroll down Main Street. I don't feel like I've actually consumed enough food for my digestive system to get working, but I do need to walk off the wine. "If you don't mind me asking, who are you going to wear to the shower tomorrow?" she asks, looking me up and down.

Who? Ah, like a designer. I go to answer, then cut short my reply. People from where I grew up don't ask each other *who* they're wearing.

I look down at the cotton summer dress I'd chosen for today's outing. It isn't going to cut it for a billionaire baby shower, is it?

"I have a little Alexander McQueen number that would be perfect, but I didn't bring it."

"Alexander McQueen? For an afternoon tea?" Her jaw drops. *The horror.* "Oh, oh you're joking, aren't you? Sorry. I've been on hiatus for a month, haven't been around any real people in a while."

Real people. I know what she means, but wow, that stings like a nasty paper cut. "People here aren't real?"

"No. Nobody who lives here's *real.* You're among the uber-rich. Claire and Ted, between them, are worth more than you can count. His family is worth more than that. Becky's dad, as well as her fiancé Chad's dad, they're billionaires, as is mine. We don't talk about it, but you need to know what you're getting into here. This isn't small fry." She loops her arm through mine as we walk along. "That's not to say there aren't a few celebrities who scrape together a few million to buy a home and then get invited to parties because of who they are, but they aren't the ones you're going to need to put in your magazine."

I know virtually nothing about these people except for what I've seen at lunch. A lot of research is going to be required before tomorrow. I'll be hitting up the internet for all the deets on the Hamptons' mega-rich inhabitants. Lifestyles of the rich and famous.

Here I am, assuming I was going to be writing about village fetes and local jams when it turns out I'm going to be mingling with the Real Housewives of the Hamptons.

"You might be right. I need to do some shopping." I reach into my bag then stop myself. *Careful, Caitlyn. You don't have money in your bank account, remember?* I throw my purse back down into the bottom of my bag. *This is awkward.*

"Would you allow me to help?" Jen grabs hold of my arm even tighter and a sense of embarrassment creeps up into me. I haven't felt this way since my mother used to have to pay for the weekly shop in pennies and coupons.

There's no way out of this without a little humor. "Ginevra Baresi, are you trying to Pretty Woman me?" *Shut up, Caitlyn.*

She laughs, thank God. "I'm not my brothers. I don't want to sleep with you in return."

"Ooh burn." My type of humor, I love it.

"I have a ton of unworn clothes at home. Every season the network sends me over a whole wardrobe of dresses and suits and I hardly ever wear any of them. You're not quite the same size as me —" I'm easily two sizes bigger and a foot shorter than she. "But I'm sure we can find you a couple of outfits."

"Thank you, that's so kind."

When I was a child I'd changed schools often, what with my mother's illness and moving in with my grandparents. Best friends were a rarity, but sometimes when I was all alone and lost in a brand-new school I came across another person who knew the school and all the other kids but they were a different kind of alone, lost in the crowd. In my experience, those people – the misfits, as some might cruelly suggest – were my kind of people.

Jen has friends, she's a successful career woman and, from memory, she's had her fair share of public relationships, and yet she smiles at me and I find a camaraderie, something I can't quite put my finger on. A new friend. Maybe it's been so long since I took my head out of a textbook that I haven't noticed that I needed one.

"And Hank gave me a credit card in case you needed to get anything. What do you say? Shall we let Hank treat you to some new shoes?" She looks down at my scruffy pumps as she says it and shakes her head. She has a point. These things belong to a previous life.

"You sure he won't mind?" Things are already awkward. I don't want him on my back for wasting the company's money too. After yesterday's shenanigans, though, am I not to some extent 'Pretty Womaning' him? *Ugh, what a horrible thought.* I had been the sensible, sober one, despite the fact that he'd been ready and willing. That has to count for something, right?

"Honey, he won't even notice." She laughs. "The card is limitless and handled by accounts who are more than used to the Baresi brothers abusing their expense accounts."

I shrug. "If you insist." And she pulls me into the kind of shop where security unlocks the door for you. Not Pretty Woman at all.

Chapter Six

Hank

In my life there are two things I can handle. One is women, and the other is liquor — at least, when it isn't mixed with my brother's illicit pills. I was born with a face that charms people into doing whatever I want them to, which normally gets me into the kind of trouble that I'd encountered on the plane two days ago.

Things I can't handle, though? *Well, how much time do you have?* Like right now at this precise moment, I can't handle kids, especially Leo's spoiled, stinky brats.

"Cut it out, Bradley." *Who calls their kid Bradley these days?* It isn't even a family name. My nephew elbows me again, then lifts his butt and farts on me. I'm this close to kicking his teenage ass and giving up my hard-earned title of favorite uncle. I always have gum. It's my thing.

"Stop fighting. Don't make me come back there." Leo thinks he is fucking hilarious, putting me in the back seat with these two. Mama and Papa, running late, had arranged for me to go in another car. I hadn't realized my pill-popping older brother was my ride until I'd sat down. We're not exactly on speaking terms.

Stuck in the back with Bradley and Peter, who I'm pretty sure filled his diaper shortly after we left, I regret not bringing my own car. But the whole gang is going to be there and I want to wet the baby's head in advance.

"Peter crapped his pants and Hank's taking up all the room."

"Am not." *Shit, I'm becoming one of them.*

The car draws up at Ted's parent's house, and my purgatory is over. The blue skies and the smell of free beer confirm that we have indeed arrived in paradise. I imagine that my brother is only passing through and he'll never get past the pearly gates. We pile out and the driver leaves, presumably with the intention of disinfecting the whole damn car.

A familiar face is waiting at the entrance to Ted's parent's garden. *What's she doing here?* I notice the camera bag on her shoulder. *Ah. She's keen.* That's either going to go in my favor or make for a very awkward office atmosphere when she finds out I don't have a clue what I'm doing.

Her cute little pink dress catches the wind and she puts her hands on her skirt to hold it down, checking around to see if anybody caught a glimpse of her matching pink lace panties. My breath hitches. I hadn't even imagined that body under yesterday's oversized T-shirt.

My eyes can't help but be drawn to her breasts, bursting out of that low neckline. I get hard thinking about them and adjust my trousers accordingly. *Come on, man. Get it together. You're supposed to have control of your dick by now.*

Her hair is all piled up on her head with little ringlets that spring down around her face in the pretty way women do when they act like they just stuck in a couple of pins but you know they probably spent three hours getting it just right. The sea breeze is working its way on knocking that down too and she ends up standing there, one hand on her skirt and the other on her head.

I quite like just admiring her from afar, as all the other guests just pass her by, but I decide to do the gentlemanly thing and rescue her.

As I approach her, my gut flips again. She does things to me that I can't explain, like I know her *intimately*.

I've never even reacted like this to a woman I've slept with, so why is a complete stranger having this effect on me? She's not my type at all, way shorter than most of the girls I date and curvier. She's an enigma, a hot, sexy enigma who I can't stop imagining naked.

I straighten my jacket and fiddle with my hair. *Should have made more of an effort.* "Caitlyn." She looks over at me and her face lights up. She could try to be a little less cute.

"Hi, did you get my message? Claire asked me to cover the shower. Well, it was Jen's idea. Isn't it exciting? Our first society article and it's here." She holds out her hand to show me Ted's parent's house as if I've never seen it before. "Their house is so beautiful. I can't wait to see the gardens." Her excitement charms me. She isn't keen to meet all the rich people. She's in awe of the surroundings, appreciating the beauty of these magnificent homes. I'll have to show her my parents' house sometime.

"I'm sorry I didn't get your message. I lost my phone on the plane." *Why did you say that? You don't have to bring it up again.* She bites her lip and looks slightly uncomfortable. Is she thinking about my dick right now?

"Shall we go through? I have to admit I'm a bit nervous. It's just that I don't know who half of the people here are."

"Well, you're in luck because I do, and I'd much rather work today than have to make small talk with these people."

"You look great, by the way. Dressed. You look great dressed. In a suit." She has this face she makes, instant chagrin whenever something dumb comes out of her mouth.

I've always had a tendency to go for women who are sure of themselves, know what they want from me and how to get it. And yet Caitlyn has this spontaneity about her, a fragility that stirs something in me. I have this strange desire to protect her. Which is why, as we enter the garden, I have a sinking feeling that I'm leading her into the lion's den.

"Uh, thank you? I do try to get dressed for these kinds of events." I'd much rather be in jeans and a T-shirt right now, although the way she's eyeing my suit, I'm obviously making an impression. I puff up my chest and hold in my gut. Give her her money's worth.

"I am so sorry. I just… I didn't mean that. I meant… You know what I meant, right?"

"Yes. I understand the confusion. I have generally been in a state of undress in your presence. How about we never speak of that again?"

"Yes, thank you. As you wish...boss man, the big boss, the man in charge." She's flustered. The words won't stop spilling out.

I interrupt her, lifting the camera bag strap from her shoulder. "Allow me. Ladies first." As she brushes past me, a hint of sweet, subtle perfume is left in her wake and my breath hitches once again. *Damn, she even smells fuckable.*

Feisty, funny and pretty goddamned attractive. Not wanting to seduce my new colleague is becoming more and more problematic.

The garden is decorated in royal blue. Ted's mother has spared no expense, literally filling the garden with blue flowers, balloons and other decorations.

Caitlyn is in awe, taking in the splendor of the occasion. "Everything here is so much bigger, more elaborate than at home."

"Well, I think this is slightly more over-the-top than any other baby showers I've had the pleasure of attending." Understatement of the century. You can't move for blue. It's blinding.

We find a quiet corner, and she prepares her camera. As she pulls it out, I notice how battered it is. *Well-loved, I suppose.* I can understand having a favorite tool. Many of mine have been mended several times or are simply held together with duct tape. But for work purposes, I had invested in something more robust than the one she holds in her hands so preciously. "That isn't the one I bought for you."

"You bought me a camera?" Her face illuminates, sending flutters through my gut.

"Yeah. I got one of Enzo's assistants to order it. I can't remember what it was called, Phase maybe?" I know jack shit about cameras. I'd just set a budget and got someone to order it.

Her jaw drops, and her hand flies to her chest. My eyes instinctively sink down to her cleavage again. I can't help it. It's just there, in my face. That dress is too fucking tight on her curves, too revealing. *Damn it.* I can't look away. I almost wish she had brought her big old T-shirt so she could just pop over it to draw my attention back to her face.

"You bought me a Phase One?"

"Maybe. I honestly don't remember." *Look in her eyes, in her eyes, Hank.*

She grasps my arm with her delicate fingers, sending a message to my groin that I do not want to reply to. "Oh my God. That is so exciting, thank you."

I've never got into a girl's panties by buying her photographic equipment, but I'm pretty sure if I throw in a tripod and a darkroom she'll be in my bed by the end of the day.

Fuck. I have to get away from this woman. It's stressing me out and making me horny.

"Sure, whatever. No problemo." Now *I'm* just spouting random shit. She has me thrown.

The gang is standing near the bar. We'll take some photos, stand a few feet apart. That's got to help. "Let's get to work."

"Caitlyn, you came. You look amazing." Claire pushes right past me and goes in for the hug. Caitlyn balks but accepts Claire's open arms. I'm no expert on body language, but I'm pretty sure she's not a hugger.

"Hi, Hank," I say, in a woman's voice. "How are you? Great thanks, Claire, and you?"

"Yeah, hi to you too. Don't think I don't know you came over and put up that furniture for Ted yesterday." I look over at Ted. We've been rumbled.

"He did it all. I just lent him the gear." I cringe and raise my hands, begging for forgiveness.

"Sure. He reinforced it too, I suppose." She raises an eyebrow.

"I got cocky," says Ted, abashed. "So you're Caitlyn? *This* is the new editor I've heard all about." I've known Ted all my life. What he'd actually said was, *'this girl is super-hot and I can see why you'd want to bang her'*.

The only other single guy in our little gang, and strangely the one that people always refer to as the 'hotter one' out of the four of us, strides over, unbuttoning his jacket and revealing a crisp, tight shirt. He ignores me too, holding out his hand for Caitlyn to shake. "Hi, nice to meet you. I'm Jonny, Hank's best friend."

Caitlyn blushes and looks coy, the standard reaction to meeting Jonny for the first time. If history is to repeat itself, then within a week she'll be cursing his name and wishing she'd never met him, like every other pretty girl who's fallen under his spell.

I might have a bit of a reputation for not settling down, but my friend here is working his way through the entire female species between the ages of eighteen and thirty.

Caitlyn pulls herself together and flashes him a very professional smile. "Nice to meet you, Jonny. I'm going to have to fix a time for us to meet up and have a chat. Your reputation precedes you."

"It does?" Jonny narrows his eyes. I know that face. He's intrigued and he's keen to know why she isn't falling at his feet. My best friend does not take kindly to women who don't want to jump into bed with him, even those who he wouldn't even consider jumping into bed with. He sees them as the ultimate challenge. And nine times out of ten he wins.

Jonny leans into her, real close, breathes in deeply, making her wait as his face hovers only an inch or so above hers and adds, "And what reputation would that be?"

"Two-time winner of the Long Island regatta," replies Caitlyn, taking a sizeable step back and checking her camera, holding it out to keep a certain distance between them.

Jonny isn't fazed. "You like seamen, huh?" He puts both hands on his hips, sticks out his chest and throws her his sexiest nod.

Jen comes up behind me and whispers, "What's going on?"

I keep my voice down to a minimum. "I think Jonny's making his move, but she's having none of it." I can't take my eyes off them. Caitlyn falling for Jonny would be a terrible idea, but I'll never date anyone he's dated. It would be the perfect antidote for the bubbling feelings inside me where this woman is concerned.

And yet, at the very same time, some part of me loves that she isn't falling for his crap. I should not sleep with Caitlyn, that is very clear, but I don't want anybody else getting their paws on her either. My protective hackles rise, although, from the looks of it, she's got this covered.

"Not really. They don't float my boat." She giggles to herself. "But I'd love a picture of you in yours for my cover," she adds, not even looking up at him.

"Did she just turn him down and flatter his ego at the same time?" asks Jen.

"Yup." My lips form a grin that I can't seem to shake off. I bite my lip.

"She's good. Love that girl. You'd best not fuck it up—or her. She's going places." I turn to look at my sister. She never likes anybody, especially anybody I've dated. *Caitlyn's won over my sister, huh?* My interest is piqued.

"Thank you. I'll do my best."

"Do better." Jen is normally on my side. *Is she finally coming around to my parents' idea of what I should be doing with my life?* I need allies right now.

Claire and Jen grab Caitlyn away from Jonny's failed clutches and pull her over to take some photos of the family and the tables before everyone sits down to eat.

"You said she was cute," says Ted. "You didn't mention that she was hot as fuck."

"And she's feisty. I love it," adds Jonny. He taps me on the back. "You fucked her yet? Because if you didn't, I'm definitely up for it."

"Dudes, please, a little respect. No, and, Jonny, I'd rather you didn't either. I need her to set up this magazine and I don't want her rushing back home because you broke her heart." I feel like I want to get to know her. I don't need these guys getting involved.

"You like her." Jonny isn't wrong. These guys know me too well, but no way am I going to tell these blabbermouths a thing.

"She's seen his cock," says Ted. And that is exactly *why* I can't trust my friends with anything.

"Who's seen whose cock?" says a voice from behind me.

Chad. The four musketeers are all here. "That's a really long story," I reply with a wink. "Anyone want a drink? I hear Ted's paying." I slap him on the back and turn to the bar. I'm not telling that story again. Nope. No way.

Chapter Seven

Caitlyn

"Are you sure you're okay with it?" Admittedly the whole 'wrong side of the road, wrong side of the car' thing is taking a bit of getting used to but I like to drive, especially this car. It had to have cost the price of a house.

"Of course. Anything has to be better than going home in my brother's car."

I tap Hank on the knee reassuringly, then instantly regret my decision when a thousand butterflies decide to have a riot inside me. "You're fine. Don't worry. I haven't killed anybody, with my driving at least. Where do I drop you off?"

"I'm staying in the house that I'm renovating. I was living in your apartment until, uh, you moved in."

He has slept in my bed — naked, splayed out, sheets draped over his naughty bits like the cover of a heavily thumbed romance novel. I take a deep breath and concentrate on the road, but there's no getting that particular image out of my head.

"Sorry about that. If you don't mind me asking, why don't you do it full-time? You talk about it, like, a lot." I've spent the afternoon with Hank, walking around, taking pictures, writing notes. The man *loves* his renovation work. Drywall, electricity, plumbing, he does it all. "Not that I mind. I actually find it very interesting. You're passionate. It's good to be enthusiastic about things." He isn't boring and has a certain charm for telling a story.

"We're not exactly hammer-and-nails type of people in my family." He shrugs his shoulders. "We do media, which means *I* do media." Jen had mentioned that he was going to lose his allowance if he didn't buck up his ideas.

My mother had never dictated anything in my life. She was what my grandmother would refer to '*as a bit of a hippie*'. I'd spent the first twelve years of my life staying up late, having picnics on the beach instead of doing my schoolwork and making daisy chains to hang around mine and my mother's necks. It was a glorious time, only marred by her crumbling health, the jarring cough that kept her awake at night, the little winces of pain, convincingly hidden most of the time and eventually the realization that our hazy days would have to come to an end. I'd been so lucky in that respect. Some people don't get that amount of love in a lifetime with their parents. I'd gotten twelve years of care and hugs and freedom.

And I'd missed it desperately every single day since, to the point where I jumped in at the deep end anytime a man showed me affection. But this time it would be different. I'm not just letting anybody in and I'm not getting hurt again. *Nope. No way.*

I look over to him. "So you created the magazine for them."

"Yes. There used to be another one, but they shut down. Dad's marketing advisor saw an opening, and I was given the opportunity to make it work."

It wasn't said with pride. Admittedly, he's had a couple of drinks, but even sober, I'm pretty sure the sarcasm in his voice would have been evident. No opportunities had been given, more like ultimatums.

"Well, *I'm* certainly glad you did." I wink at him. *Shit.* That came out way flirtier than I'd intended. I've been fighting my attraction to Hank all afternoon — the fitted suit, top button undone on his shirt, tie loosened. I hadn't intended to sound so seductive, but there's a real possibility that his expensive aftershave is intoxicating me. "Because of the job, obviously."

He grins, that seductive, pussy-melting smile, and turns to look at me as he speaks. "Me too."

"But you want to do it, right? You're in this for the long haul."

He tips his head to one side, hesitates a long time before replying. "Sure." I'm not so sure. The passion in his voice when he talks about renovation is far more pointed than when he mentions the magazine. In fact, he's hardly mentioned it all day. "This is me." He points to a driveway and I draw up in front of it. The house is gorgeous — wood built and painted bright white, as many are in this area, surrounded by a perfectly tended garden.

"It's beautiful." And expensive. According to my research, houses around here go for at least a few million, then there are the top-class fixtures and fittings. No wonder he needs the money to complete it.

"Want to take a look around?" The way he says it, it's almost like he's asking me back for 'coffee' after a date. I really ought to say no.

"I'd love to." I park in the driveway. Clearly my mouth didn't get the memo.

The ground floor is an open-plan living area. Dining room, kitchen and living room all in one, just like my apartment. The back of the house is one long set of glass doors, leading out to the garden and pool. It's beautifully finished.

"Come on through. I have something amazing to show you."

I look down at my high heels. The floor is littered with paint pots, tools and all other kinds of necessary house doing-up type things. "Uh, maybe I should have changed my shoes." It isn't that I'm too girly, quite the opposite, I've already tripped and slipped several times today. I miss my flat shoes. This place is a veritable minefield that I will not make across in one piece.

"I got you." He wraps his two strong arms, very delicately, around my legs and body and he pulls me to his chest. That aftershave again. *Good God, man, a woman can only resist so much.* I close my eyes and try to stop my nether regions from holding a Thanksgiving parade. My nipples betray me in a way that nipples only can when a man's hands are on my body. Thank God for heavy-duty push-up bras.

He steps over everything and carries me right to the back of the house. Behind the kitchen a small hallway leads to another room. He puts me down, gently, but my damned heels and flustered body fail me. I stumble back against the window, narrowly missing a large pot of wood varnish.

Once again his arms are around me, holding me in a sweeping embrace. "You okay?" Our faces only inches apart, we freeze, staring into each other's eyes, contemplating. Kissing this man would be very, *very*, wrong. He is my boss.

And yet, in that very second, we both abandon any illusion of platonic feelings. This is exactly how it had happened on the plane. A touch of turbulence had sent my drunken body reeling into his. And the rest was history.

Without hesitation, our lips come together. He kisses me, and I kiss him. A mutual impulse that neither of us can deny. It is delicious, warm, sweet bourbon for the soul, as if destiny is absolutely insisting we find each other and continuously throws me into his arms until we get it right.

He pulls away and stares at me. Does he remember? He seems confused. His eyes narrow, scanning my face. We'd kissed that night on the plane, but it wasn't sweet and romantic like this. That had been wanton, lust-filled, drunken making out, the type of kiss you have to wipe off of your face when you've finished.

"I am *so* sorry. I don't know what came over me." I have no excuse, except an entirely warranted desire to fuck this beautiful man. But I'm supposed to be a grown-up. Then there's the whole *he's my boss* thing. *Remember that, Caitlyn?* Plus, Hank is Mr. Wrong, the naked cowboy from the plane, the perfect example of the type of man I should not be kissing. He doesn't even remember that he'd nearly fucked me.

"No, it's me who should be apologizing. I'm obviously drunker than I thought. That was totally inappropriate." He looks seriously panicked. His parents finding out he's snogged the new editor would make a frosty situation downright chilly.

"How about we just forget this ever happened? I'm jetlagged, and you're a little tipsy. Let's put it down to unfortunate circumstances and never mention it again."

The list of things that we are never mentioning again grows daily. I'm going to have to fill in a Post-it Note and stick it somewhere so I remember exactly what I can and can't discuss with the man.

I know me. I know I will cogitate, re-think and analyze this for eternity. Plus, I am already having some serious fantasies about this man's fingers on my pussy, under the sheets, with no clothes on. But he doesn't need to know that.

"Sure, yeah. Cool." He steps back, and opens the door. "I wanted to show you the uh, the master bedroom." A bedroom? He really isn't helping the situation whatsoever.

"It looks amazing." It does. The back wall is covered in fitted bookshelves, filled entirely with books. If his kisses don't finish me off, this certainly will. A man after my own heart.

"You read. *A lot.*" The number of books on those shelves fills my heart with joy. I almost forget he is there for a second. I want to read all of them, but where to begin?

"Yeah, I spend most of my time in half-finished houses with no electricity and before that, I used to travel, so I'd often find myself alone in my hotel room." If this man is trying to stop my juices from flowing, he is going about it very much the wrong way. Books, literature. That's *my* passion. When I'm not reading, I'm writing.

"I love it, I really do. I gave all my books away before moving here." I walk over to the shelves and peruse his collection. "I might have to borrow a few of these." Who am I kidding? I'm moving in. I'm giving him no choice in the matter. He can have the apartment with the tiny library. This right here is my new home.

"Be my guest. Anyway, this is what I actually wanted to show you, the *pièce de résistance*." He's not going to get this dick out again, is he? Why did that thought enter my mind? Probably because I can still taste him on my lips. Ugh, the struggle is real.

He presses a button on the wall and two panels on the ceiling recede to reveal a large window. "It's to watch the stars." He bites his lip and waits for my reaction, fidgeting with nervous excitement.

I suddenly see Hank—not the drunk hunk from the plane, the guy trying to please his parents to keep the cash flowing or even the irresistibly handsome man in a suit. The person in front of me is doing what we all do at some point in our lives. Seeking validation.

Like a kid who shoves their artwork under their parents' noses, '*Mum, look, I drew this*', Hank is showing me his handiwork. *Is it possible that nobody else had seen this house, this room? Fuck. That sucked.*

"I love it." I walk over to the bed. I can imagine lying in bed with someone looking up at the stars at night. You'd have to be a bit of a romantic to create that. I look at Hank. Yeah, I can see it. "May I?"

"Yes."

I plump up a pillow and sit down, patting the space next to me. "Come. Sit. Tell me about your plans for this place."

"You sure?"

"Sure I want to talk, or sure I'm not going to jump you?" I can't guarantee it. One whiff of his aftershave and I might lose it. His face is priceless. "I'm kidding. I think we've established that we can behave like grown-ups if we really try, right? Come on."

He sits, talks. I listen. Nobody jumps anybody.

Ever so slowly, the stars appear above us.

There are moments in your life which you look back upon and can pinpoint as '*the moment when*'. Without a single doubt, that night was the moment when I fell in love with Enrico Baresi.

Chapter Eight

Hank

Monday morning. Normally, I have to drag myself out of bed with the promise of coffee and a shower, but I've been awake for an hour, just staring at the sky.

I tap the pillow next to me. It still smells like Caitlyn. She'd stayed until late Saturday, just listening, chatting, trying to remember the constellations.

That kiss. Shit. I haven't stopped reliving it since her perfect lips landed on mine. I mean, yeah, she's right. We can't go there. *But fuck, it was good.* She tasted like cotton candy. That dress, the way her body felt in my arms. It was almost as if… It sounds wild, but as if she knew exactly how I like to be kissed.

My loins stir. I'm seriously having trouble keeping this guy down at the moment.

I grab my cock as if to chastise it. I have to stop thinking about her in that way. A quick shower then off to my first day of work. *Eyes on the goal, Hank. Eyes on the goal.*

* * * *

"Caitlyn?" I try not to look like she hasn't left my mind since the last time I saw her.

"Good morning," she sings, popping up from under the kitchen counter. "I was looking for biscuits. Cookies. Digestives?"

"Digestives? I don't know…"

"No matter. I made coffee. It took a YouTube tutorial and three attempts, but it no longer looks like dishwater and it smells divine. It's all in the tapping down. I don't know if that's the technical term." The words are spilling out of her mouth again. "How do you like it?" She's wearing a dress again. This one is less formal than yesterday's, more summery. I've never noticed someone's clothing so much. I'm so distracted by her I don't even listen to what she's saying. In fact, I have no idea what she just said. She holds up a coffee mug. *Ah.*

"Black, no sugar."

"Cool. Okay. That I can do." She hands me a mug and throws me another wide grin. She's chirpy for eight a.m.

"So, what's the plan for today?" Journalism 101? How to convince your parents and your one very talented employee that you know what the fuck you're doing?

"I made a list of everything I need to know. Then I made a list of everybody I want to interview or visit, in the case of local businesses. If you don't mind, I'd like you to see if you can make me a list of events and mark them on the calendar." She grabs her own coffee and walks over to a wall of whiteboards. "Calendars are here. I'll write where we both are every day here, just so you know at a glance, where you're supposed to be on any given day."

"Okay." The whiteboards are covered in lists and Post-its and calendars. Perfectly organized. I need one of these on-site, the number of times I've forgotten about a delivery or a contractor. I'm not someone you can count on to remember a birthday or an anniversary. A year of business college taught me that I'm no good at presenting projects within a specific timeline or anything that involves the least bit of organization on my part. Someone wants me to calculate how many tiles they need for their bathroom or your kitchen? I can do that in my head. How much paint am I going to need to redo a living room, I've worked that out in a second. If we arranged to go out two weeks ago, though, I'm going to need that person to send me a reminder by text, if I can still find my phone.

"I know this should probably all need to be digital or something, but I have to visualize these things so they enter my brain. Does that make sense?"

"Yeah. I get it." Caitlyn reads real books, she takes photos, she writes lists and pins up Post-it notes. I can understand that. We're standing in a room I've rebuilt, on a floor I've laid. We are people who need things, real actual things, to help us function. I find myself smiling at her as she talks, understanding how her mind works.

"Mornings are going to be dedicated to interviews and visits, afternoons to writing. I plan to launch the website the beginning of July, paper version in September, at the end of the season."

"Perfect. What do you need from me?" *Please let it be filing.* I can do filing. Or making coffee, because I'm smiling, but this is like tar in a mug.

"I'm going to need you in the office on the mornings when I'm out, and I'll need you to accompany me to events, until I get to know who's who. Otherwise, you're free every afternoon" — she hesitates — "to do what makes you happy." She flashes me a conspiratorial smile.

How have I gotten so fucking lucky? This woman has traveled across continents to work for me. She's seen me at my very worst and brushed it off as a joke. She accepts my passion and sees me for who I really am. *Are all Brits like this, or have I just stumbled across the most perfect woman in all of England?*

"What kinds of events do you need to know about? While that's not really my thing, I know just the person to help you." *Mama.* At sixty-five years old, my mama has lived a lifetime of socializing. She had moved to New York when they were married and they'd bought their first Hamptons house just before Enzo was born. Papa grew up over here, Mama in Italy. There are very few social events that she doesn't know about. She has a circle of friends that includes some of the most exclusive families on the island.

"Could you fix us up a meeting with them?"

"I can do better. We'll go have lunch with her. I'll give her a call. We'll start making our way through your lists and then we'll go see my mama."

Caitlyn gulps loudly. "Your mama?"

"Don't worry. She's a sweetheart. And don't tell the rest of my family, but I'm her favorite." It's hardly a secret. The surprise sixth baby. I've broken my poor mother's heart a million times, but she always forgives me.

* * * *

Mama waited for us at the door, beautiful as always. Her long black hair pinned up in a neat bun, almost hiding that striking streak of gray, which is about the only thing that gives away her age.

"Is your mother a model?"

"Mama? She was an actress in Italy. She met my father when she was working in New York."

She welcomes us, arms wide open. "Enrico, *il mio figlio. Sei molto magro,* you are too thin. You don't eat." This again. My father insisted that my siblings and I were brought up by nannies. It is what it is when you're rich. He showed her the world and we would stay at home, under the watchful eye of our fair-weather caregivers. So when Mama was there, she insisted we eat pasta for lunch and pasta for dinner. Feeding us is her way of showing us she loves us and she loves us *a lot.*

"I do nothing but eat. Trust me." I try to pinch an inch of fat, but she has a point, I've been working on my renovation night and day recently and I may have skipped a meal or two. "Mama, this is Caitlyn, my new colleague."

"*Si, si, benvenuto.* Welcome to our home."

"*Piacere di conoscerti,* Mrs. Baresi, I hope I said that right."

"You speak Italian?" asks my mother. *Caitlyn speaks Italian? What?* I try to hide my surprise. I really should have read her CV when they'd hired her. I feel like there's a lot to know about Caitlyn that I have yet to learn.

"*Solo un po.*" Caitlyn does the international, pinched-finger hand-signal for 'only a little'.

"You call me Mama. Everyone calls me Mama."

Caitlyn nods.

"Mama, these are for you." She hands over a simple bouquet that she had insisted on buying on the way over.

Mama's hand taps her chest with delight. "*Dolce, bambino,* you bring me flowers. In Italy we give flowers. It is traditional. Nobody visits without giving flowers. Here in America they don't give flowers. They give you macaroni and cheese, but it is not macaroni. It is poison." Mama throws her hands up in disgust, then smells her bouquet and smiles at her guest.

Caitlyn turns and winks at me. So that's why we *had* to buy flowers.

"Shall we eat? I'm starving," I say. My mother leads us through the house to the garden.

"Is this where you grew up?" Caitlyn is like a wide-eyed tourist in the Sistine Chapel. My parents' house is wildly ornate. As far as I can recall, a lot of the decoration has been copied from Italian renaissance homes. There is enough marble to recreate the Taj Mahal. It is not to my taste, but my childhood memories were formed within these walls and I love it.

"Only in the summer and on weekends, otherwise we lived in New York."

"This is your holiday cottage?"

"I guess so." My friends tease me about being well-traveled. They see those three years that I spent abroad as being one long party with a bit of surfing and sex in between. They aren't far from the truth in many respects, but I've seen things they haven't seen. How the other ninety-nine percent lives. And it marked me.

I turn to Caitlyn and look into her eyes, wondering if I should share how I really feel about this place. I know she gets me, somehow, more than my closest friends, but I don't want to come off as pretentious. "I couldn't ever live in a house like this again, or drive a car that cost a million dollars. I love my friends and family and I'm not about to shun them because of who they are, but you can't live in a tent in the Tunisian desert for three months, drinking goats' milk and learning how to live on virtually nothing and then come back and act like this is normal."

There's nothing philanthropic about it. I'm not planning to sponsor a hospital wing or save the whales. I just want to flip my houses and live my life.

"You did that? Amazing. You'll have to dig out some pictures and we'll stick it online sometime. *Travels with Enrico.* I can see it now." The sincerity in her reply confirms my belief that I had nothing to worry about. She gets me.

As usual, my mother can't help herself. The table on the terrace is laid for a three-course meal. I'd said just a sandwich and a salad would do, but Mama Baresi can never resist filling up my 'skinny' stomach every time she sees me.

"Sit, sit. Tell me all about you, *tesoro.* Where are you from?"

"I grew up in London, living with my grandmother. My mother died when I was twelve—"

"I didn't know that," I say, interrupting her, then catching myself and sitting back, encouraging her to finish.

She flashes a reassuring smile. "You weren't to know. It was a long time ago." Fifteen years, if my calculation is correct. Around the same time that I lost my poppa and that still hurt to this day. I couldn't imagine if it were my own mother.

"Oh, I'm so sorry for your loss." She places her hand on Caitlyn's. "Did you know my husband's mother lives with us? Nonna is ninety years old. She helped raise all our children."

"Oh goodness, what a blessing to still have her around." She goes to say something else but bites her tongue. The more I learn about Caitlyn, the more I think she is not just some girl from London. I think back to when I met Caitlyn, how quickly the air had turned blue. I can hardly believe she's the same woman, sitting next to me in a sweet little summer dress, exclaiming so politely. *Goodness* and *Gosh*.

"Nonna surprises everyone. That woman will outlive us all," replies my mother, with a tinge of insincerity. Nobody can argue that my grandmother is a sweet old woman. She has a fiery character and a loud bark, of which my mother is normally on the receiving end.

"Where is she?" I ask.

"She's out dancing. Well, of course, she doesn't dance as much these days. She just likes to go and beat everybody else at Canasta." Nonna has been the belle of the ball most of her life, and an important figure in Hamptons society. If I live even half the life she has, I won't complain.

"This is one of the things I'd love to cover for the magazine. Real people, real lives. Your mother-in-law sounds like such a character. I'd love to meet her."

"We should go see her today." Is it Caitlyn's influence, this impulsivity? First, I'm inviting her to lunch with Mama and now I'm offering to go see Nonna. Or is it just that I want to spend every minute with her? I'm doing my best to behave like an adult, as promised, and yet I want to be next to her, close to her all the time.

"Can we? Oh, I would love to. We'll have to get my camera from the office. What a lovely idea."

"But first, you must eat," says Mama, handing me a basket of bread rolls. "Soup, then pasta, then your favorite lemon cheesecake."

I have to admit that my first day of working for a living is turning out to be much better than I'd expected. I could get used to this.

Chapter Nine

Caitlyn

Hank's mother is a delight. She filled up my social calendar for the next few weeks. It looks like Hank and I are going to be spending quite a few weekends sipping free expensive champagne all over the Hamptons. The perks of the job. And the company is not the worst either.

Despite my early concerns, Hank is turning out to be a pretty good coworker. He's keen to do what we need to get this little enterprise up and running. And he's certainly putting in the effort today.

I've relived that kiss in my mind a million times since it happened, letting my imagination wander as to what would have happened if we'd just let ourselves go. Would I have been simply another notch on the bedpost? Would I be in his arms right now? Who knows? Some things are better laid to rest.

If only my body would be so kind as to agree with my mind. The simple act of sitting next to him in the car or at the lunch table is sending my blood pressure through the roof. He has a certain charisma, like a hormone, that seeps out of his pores and seduces with just a subtle glance. Logic is fighting it off for now, but I'm going to need something more than that if I'm going to survive the rest of my working life resisting his charms.

His parents' relationship intrigues me. The other day at the baby shower I'd gotten a headache trying to keep up with who was who—divorces, remarriages, double-barreled names. It was a nightmare. "Can I ask you something?"

"Shoot."

"Your parents, they've been married for, what, forty years?"

"Yeah." He stretches it out, wary of what I'm *actually* asking, maybe.

"Is that normal here? I just assumed billionaires got divorced all the time and married younger women."

He laughs and rubs his forehead in despair. "Why?"

"Because they can."

"No, why did you think that?" Personal experience, but I'm not ready to share that. I give him the answer that he expects from someone like me.

"I don't know…TV, movies, celebrity websites." Cheap magazines called *Yeah* and *Wowzers* that you found in the dentist's waiting room.

"Well, my parents' friends are littered with divorced and remarried couples, sure, but isn't it like that for everybody?"

"I know a lot of people who've gotten divorced, but I don't know many men who remarried with women half their age. Does that happen a lot?"

"Yeah. It's not uncommon." He lifts his eyebrows and tilts his head to one side, questioning my motives. "Are you suggesting that's what my dad should have done?"

Is he teasing me or being serious? I can't tell.

Perfect, now he thinks that I think his mother is old and replaceable. "Oh God no, your mum is beautiful and amazing. He'd be crazy to let her go."

Hank grins at me like the proud son that he is, letting his gaze linger a little too long. "Thank you."

"Eyes on the road, Mr. Baresi. Six kids too. Your mother is a saint. I couldn't even imagine. No, thank you."

"You don't want kids?" Eek. That's a first date question I avoid like the plague, and we're only supposed to be work colleagues.

"It's something I thought I wanted, when I was younger, but now — I don't know. I definitely don't want six. That's for sure." *Can you even imagine?* I can hardly look after myself.

"I've yet to meet a woman who didn't have either marriage or kids on her future wish list." Well, welcome to my dreadful love life.

"I've yet to meet a man who didn't pale at the first sign of commitment, and if I'm not mistaken, you fall under that category too, Mr. I Don't Date I Just Sleep with Models." His cheeks redden. I've hit a sore point.

His grin is forced. "Who told you that? My sister? Whoever it is, they're wrong. I dated an actress once." My shocked gasp makes him laugh. "I'm kidding. That really isn't true, you know."

"I'm a journalist, I have my sources. Anyway, I've had enough of cheats and liars. That's basically my dating backlist, with the occasional utter bastard thrown in for good measure."

"You? I find that hard to believe." My turn to give him a smile, coy though it is.

"Cheats, liars, weirdoes, I've dated them all." I hesitate, bite my tongue for once. This isn't something I talk about. My terrible taste in men is my problem, but it's also a reflection on me. I might not want to take action on the feelings that are stirring inside me, but I don't want Hank to think badly of me either.

"Like what?"

Despite my hesitation, my mouth operates independently from my brain. "One boyfriend had sex with my friend in the kitchen while I slept on the sofa."

"Holy shit."

Yeah. I know.

"I woke up and went searching for him. Spent a whole minute with my hand on the kitchen door handle, trying to decide whether I wanted to know what they were doing."

"And?"

"Curiosity killed the cat." Hank snarls and shakes his head.

"Fuck." He pats me on the knee. "I apologize for mankind. We suck. Sorry."

"Then there was the guy who flirted with everybody in front of me, like a game. He'd bet me whether he could get a girl's number, even though I was right there."

"No fucking way. I don't even want to know. Yes I do. Did he get her number?"

"Yup."

"Holy fuck, Caitlyn. You sure do pick them." I blame my mother entirely, very little television and a daily visit to the library. She'd filled my head with flowery romantic idealism, making the world seem like the Garden of Eden. She hadn't mentioned there would be snakes.

"Right? What about you? Ever get your heart broken?"

"Nah. Never gave it to anybody. Well, I guess, maybe once. Becky. Then I found out she was sleeping with Chad. That stung." Wow. Becky gets around. Hank curls his lips up into a sneer. Something about this conversation is dredging up some strong emotions for him.

"And you're still friends with them?"

"Yeah. I just, you know… I just hate it when people cheat."

"Well, I guess karma came back to bite Chad in the butt." *Shit. Shut up, Caitlyn.*

"What? Why?"

Fuck, fuck, fuck. "What? Nothing. I'm sure it's nothing. I don't know." Jesus, though, you have to be blind not to see it.

"What do you know, Caitlyn Walsh?" The way he pronounces my name, it melts me, like he's so well-spoken most of the time but my name brings out this accent. I don't know New York, maybe? It tickles me, and I love it.

I know I shouldn't, but I can't resist. "Well, uh, she's uh, I might be wrong, but I'm pretty sure she's sleeping with Jonny."

His jaw drops for about ten seconds, then he laughs, like a bitter cackle. "You're kidding me? What? Who told you that?"

"Oh, nobody had to. It's so obvious. Really, you can't see it?" Sometimes I wonder if men are even the same species as us women. The sexual tension around those two is, well, about as blatant as the sexual tension between me and Hank, only theirs is more of an afterthought, not wishful thinking.

"No." He takes on a serious tone." You know they're getting married in July, right? Fuck, I hope you're wrong." That look again, on his face. This man does not like a cheater.

"Me too. Wow. Sorry. Really, I didn't mean to offend. I've probably got it all wrong. I hardly know them." I'd bet every penny I have that Jonny is boning Becky, but whatever, I don't know them like Hank does.

He shrugs his shoulder, puts a reassuring hand on my knee. "Don't be. It's probably a cultural thing. That's all."

"Yeah." He draws up at the dance hall, thank God. If this conversation goes on any longer, he'll have to pass me a rope to pull myself out of this massive hole I've dug for myself.

Chapter Ten

Caitlyn

"Have you fucked him yet?" She squints at me, balancing precariously on a barstool, ill-fitting wig on her head. Hank's grandmother has decided that an interrogation is in order.

"I'm sorry?"

"I said have you fucked him yet? Are you deaf, girl?" Her Italian accent is strong, but she speaks perfect English, sounding almost like one of those women from the films my grandmother used to watch.

"No." I swallow my intimidation. "No, I'm not deaf and no, I haven't fucked him yet."

She takes a puff on her cigarette holder. Inhaling right down to her gut. Then she blows out smoke rings, one by one, watching them float away.

"Good, well, don't get any ideas."

"We almost did, once, but he was so high he doesn't remember. I do, though. I remember every single second of it. Are you allowed to smoke in here?"

She raises one solitary, penciled-in eyebrow and blows a smoke ring in my face.

"What are they going to do, arrest me? I'm pretty sure we own the place."

I resist the urge to cough. "I thought you came here to play Canasta and dance."

"I come here to drink dry martinis and escape my dreary daughter-in-law."

"Well then…" I sit down on the stool next to her and address the barman. "Two dry martinis please." For the first time since I started talking to her, Nonna throws me a smile, her face creasing into a million nicotine-stained wrinkles.

"Where's the boy?"

"He's taking down the names of people I photographed for an article. The music's loud and nobody in this place can hear. He'll be a while." At least long enough for a martini and a chat with his dear, sweet grandma.

"Why didn't you fuck him?"

"Are you always so interested in your grandchildren's love lives?"

"Only when they sleep with the help."

The help? Okay.

I smile politely. "Because he was too drunk. I didn't want to take advantage."

"What are you, Mother Theresa?"

If only she knew.

"In my defense, I had no idea he was my boss at the time." I fell onto him and he fell on my mouth. It's not science.

"Sure. You didn't notice the platinum card in his wallet. Or the suit on his back."

"Surprisingly, no. I do now, though. Do you think if I fuck him tonight I'll get a diamond ring and a fur coat?" I pause for effect. "Or maybe I should hold out until he gives me my own platinum card. I really can't decide." I twirl my olive around the glass then suck the liquor off it.

"You think you're smart? Nothing ever comes from people like us sleeping with people like you."

"Tried it, have you?" That shook her. Nonna had secrets. "And yes. I'm very smart indeed and it's not 1950 anymore. People don't just sleep with peasants these days. They get ironclad prenups and marry them."

She purses her lips, contemplating her next move, or maybe just getting her dentures in place before replying.

"Twice. Once, during the war, they sent the men who wouldn't fight to work in our stables. Severino, he stayed on when the fighting was over. He read me poetry in between mucking out the horses. We made hay, as you say." She looked away. "Father had him beaten and sent away. Then, once again, later. My husband was a good man, but he worked so hard that he was never there. I think he knew. He never said it, but I saw it in his eyes."

"Did you love them?"

She toys with her glass. "Does it matter?"

"No. I suppose not, if you were happy." Her thin bony fingers wrap around her glass so tightly I'm scared she'll break it, but Hank joins us before she can reply.

"Nonna, I see you've met Caitlyn. She's working on my magazine with me."

"That's wonderful, darling." She takes a final, long puff on her cigarette, burning it to the stub and downs her drink. "Dance with me."

I stay at the bar, sip the rest of my drink. Holy crap. If Nonna is anything to go by, meeting Hank's dad is going to be a ball.

* * * *

"What do you want to do to celebrate our first day's work? A drink? You want to go eat something? I know a great place that sells lobster rolls. My treat." Our first day of work has so far involved having lunch with Hank's mom and drinking martinis with Hank's grandmother. Okay, I'm the one who had been drinking, but still, it hasn't been as productive as it could have been. I suppose the second part of the day, as I got some photos and a couple of interviews, might be considered work, but only at a stretch. Hank seems happy enough, though, and he's the boss.

"Oh well, if you're treating. I wouldn't mind seeing the beach. I've already been here a few days and I've yet to see these sandy beaches everyone raves about. Maybe a beach bar that does simple food."

"I know just the place."

We park at a beautiful white wooden building on the seafront. It looks like a glorified boathouse, but I'm coming to learn that buildings in the Hamptons are never quite what they seem.

Inside it is a beautifully decorated hotel, classic and simple but so very elegant. A waiter takes us through and out onto a deck with the most gorgeous sea view.

"I should warn you," Hank says, rather embarrassed, "it's open mic night tonight. That means you could sit here and listen to some great music, or you might have to put up with some, uh, not so great music."

Inside I'm jumping up and down for joy, but I try my best to hide it. I love music. The number of evenings I'd spent around a campfire with my mother, strumming my guitar, listening to her sing? Those were the memories I missed the most. I didn't much have the heart to pick up my guitar these days.

"Ooh, I love it," I reply, rubbing my hands together in glee. "Can anybody join in?"

Hank looks horrified. "I don't really know…"

"Oh go on," I add. "I'll sing for you."

I'm not quite sure whether this makes it better or worse. He's only known me twenty-four hours and I'm already offering to serenade him. I guess that would put most people off of their dinner. "Okay, if you really want to. It's your night out."

I could hug him right now. "Yay, thank you, thank you."

Chapter Eleven

Hank

I am not a fan of open mic night. I don't know if Caitlyn's quite understands what it's like to sit in a restaurant and be forced to listen to amateur musicians who can't get a real gig.

She's thrilled, though, fidgeting excitedly in her seat, and the food in this place is great, so I'll have to console myself with decent lobster and a table as far away from the stage as possible.

We're seated in the far corner of the deck. It cost me a few bucks extra in the waiter's hand to get it, but I'm sure whoever reserved it will turn on their heels when they realize it's open mic night, anyway. The seats are like little benches backed up against the balcony and I get to stretch out my arms and relax. It's been a good first day, and Caitlyn is great company. She talks like nobody I have ever met in my life, words just barreling out of her mouth, quite often ones that should have stayed inside and stewed a bit first.

Her openness, her excitement about everything, it's like the world is just one big discovery. I'm the same age as her but she makes me feel jaded, cynical. I used to be like that when I traveled, but I've been home for a few years now and everything feels the same. The people, life in general.

She's growing on me, stirring something inside me. That doesn't happen to me very often. Normally I'm quick to find fault, but Caitlyn's 'faults' are quirks that charm me. I'm growing soft.

We order drinks and a shared starter while we peruse the menu. I'm not hungry, really. I just wanted an excuse to spend more time with her.

"Excuse me," says Caitlyn, placing her hand on the waiter's arm as he delivers our food, "are there any free slots tonight for the open mic?"

"There are five slots, three of which are taken. Why? Would you like one?"

"Yes please, but I'll need an acoustic guitar. Is that something that could be arranged?"

"Of course, no problem, you go on in about an hour." He nods and winks in an overfriendly manner. He's probably not flirting with her, it's just his job, but it doesn't sit well with me either way. *I'm right here, dude. She's not my girlfriend, but she could be and you don't know that.*

"So, you sing then?" I ask as Mr. Seduction walks away.

"Yes. My mum taught me to play the guitar when I was little. Is that a problem, me doing the open mic thing? I love singing. Sorry. I got a bit ahead of myself."

I want to tell her I hate it, that I'd rather cut off my ears than listen to amateur singers all night, but her excitement is contagious and she deserves to enjoy herself tonight.

"Sure. You'd better be good, though." She looks over at me and frowns, then catches my smile and laughs. That's the kind of thing I say to my friends, not colleagues. My guard is down, and I like it.

"I am, I think. I haven't had any complaints. I used to love singing in public. Busking for fun in town on a Saturday."

"Busking?"

"Singing for money. That's one of the reasons, I'm sure, that my mum taught me to play in the first place. The cute kid with the guitar, tugging at people's heart and purse strings. Can't do it anymore, though." A blush rises in her cheeks.

"Why?" She grabs a bread roll and breaks it up.

"My grandmother would have killed me. Shameful behavior." She widens her eyes and drops her jaw, mimicking her grandmother's distaste. I get it. My parents gave me the same look when I said I was going into construction. Looks like Caitlyn and I have more in common than we think.

We share our food and talk about musical tastes. Apparently, I don't have any. She's musing about Seventies rock bands and Nineties pop, and I'm here saying I liked Coldplay's last song. She knows her stuff. The more time I spend with her, talking and sharing, the less I see her as just some girl I'd like to fuck.

I still want to bang her. My dick hasn't dropped off since I saw her in that pink dress. Forbidding myself from getting involved with her is allowing me to get to know her and I've never done that before. Women have always been a friend or a sexual partner, never have the two things overlapped. Says a lot about the man I've become, I guess.

"You're up next." Mr. Loverboy is back, guitar in hand, smiling in an overfriendly manner at Caitlyn. *Stop ogling her.*

She squeezes my arm, a nervous smile on her face. "Wish me luck."

"Break a leg." I take her hand in mine. She's shaking. I wink at her and tighten my grip. "You've got this. Go bask or busk or whatever."

"Okay." She giggles, pulls away to grab the guitar from Mr. Seduction. My hand feels empty.

Please, *please* don't be terrible.

After a couple of minutes tuning the guitar, she launches into a song. I'm nervous for her. Turns out she's folksy, a little bit country. She serenades us with an Irish folk song, catching the audience's attention after all the shouty crooners we've had to sit through up until now.

She handles the guitar like it's part of her. What else can she do with those fingers? And her voice, not great, but raspy and soft and soothing, like a mother singing a lullaby.

I'm enchanted by this woman. She's not perfect. Some things she excels at and others pass her by. Her camera and that guitar are handled with such ease and yet she drives like the road is going to jump out at her.

I'm sitting here watching her sing to a room full of strangers, but when it comes to taking down people's names for photos, that's my job. She hates it, gets nervous in crowds. She's an enigma to me, a strange new being. All kinds of emotional shit is stirring inside me and I don't know what to do with it.

I think my relationship status just got changed to, *it's complicated.*

Chapter Twelve

Hank

Growing up, my parents used religion constantly in reference to how good or bad my siblings and I were, but I'm not a churchgoer like them. I still pray when everything is going to shit and more often than not the Big Man's name is used in vain, especially when I'm watching a Mets game, but I'm not one to worship.

"Why exactly are we going to a church?" I yawn and stretch in my seat, filling the car and making Caitlyn duck. Mornings are not my strong point.

"For its unique architectural structure."

"Huh?" Five a.m. is way too early for big words. "And why so early?"

"To catch the sunrise as it shines through the stained-glass windows. A different perspective. A new day dawns on the Hamptons. Nobody is ever in a church at sunrise."

"True. And why did I have to come?" This has to come under the category of, *things she can do on her own*. I need my beauty sleep.

"You didn't. I thought it might make a change from sitting in the office twiddling your thumbs."

"At five a.m.?" What's the real reason?

Caitlyn sighs and waves her hand in exasperation. "I'll buy you breakfast afterwards."

She parks the car and grabs her camera. She hasn't stopped fiddling with the thing since she found out I'd bought it for her. Money well spent.

"Oh, it's the red building. I've been here before. Well, I've driven past this place. It's a church?" It looks like a house. Houses are big around here. I guess the crosses on the spires should have given it away.

We get out and walk up to the front door. Caitlyn had called in advance, bandied the Baresi name around and got them to leave a lockbox on the door for us. She's only been working for me a couple of days and she's already filled her calendar for the next two weeks like a little spitfire, always signing up to photograph some event or report on a new business that's opened.

"The stained-glass windows were made by Tiffany." She is so excited about this, pointing them all out, running over and inspecting them individually. They're impressive works of art. She sets up her tripod and positions her camera. The sun rises, beams shine through the windows, the place illuminates. It's beautiful, humbling. You can't fault her. She was right about how amazing it would be.

I perch on a pew, unsure if that's allowed when there's no service or you're not in prayer. "There's something so ethereal about these places."

"Churches? I've only ever been in a church three times. Two funerals and a wedding." She smiles wryly. "Sounds like a movie."

"You've only ever been to a wedding once in your life?"

She laughs. "No, silly. I was only young when my mum died. The church was freezing. I remember being hugged by a lot of people I didn't know and just wanting to leave. I didn't go to churches after that. Got quite a reputation for only going to receptions and never sitting through the church ceremony. My grandmother would leave me outside in the car."

"I'm sorry about your mom." There are very few women in my life, apart from family, who I've ever cared to know anything about. In the short time I've known her, she's already shared so much about herself. She talks constantly, so a lot of it's down to that, but there's an ease between us, a sense of trust.

"It was a long time ago."

"So who got married?" Please don't let it be her.

"My father." Caitlyn joins me on the pew, settling down next to me, her hands on her lap. "I got an invitation in the post. My grandmother insisted I had to go. I stood at the front of another cold church and watched my father marry a complete stranger to me. Then I was hugged by a lot of people I didn't know and I left."

I grab her hand, instinctively, and she looks down at our palms entwined then back up at me. I realize now why I'd been dragged out of bed at an ungodly hour. She wanted company. "American churches are warm," I say. My sentence is loaded with words unsaid.

"They are. I might try one sometime. Are you religious?"

"I'm Italian." It's probably written somewhere in Italian law that we all have to be Catholic. Makes no sense otherwise. I certainly don't know any Italians who aren't at least baptized.

"True. But do you believe in the Big Man?"

Good question.

"Dangerous question to ask in a church. What if he strikes me down if I say no?"

"Then logic dictates that you were wrong." She winks at me. "I like to think there's somewhere else, something after all this. Maybe because in twenty-seven years, all of this has been a bit of shit, really. Don't get me wrong. I'm not complaining. I just thought it would get a bit easier by now."

"Maybe you needed to go to a place with warm churches." I tighten my grip, lacing my fingers through hers, and gaze down into those beautiful brown eyes. "And warm hands."

She giggles. "Enrico Baresi, are you trying to seduce me in a church?" That accent again, doing things to my gut.

"No." *Maybe. Am I?*

Her smile drops and she takes on a more serious tone. "You're considering it though, aren't you? Seducing me."

"Yes." This place is so peaceful and calming it makes me want to sit here all day, flirting sweetly with Caitlyn, her hand in mine.

"I'm pretty sure that's not allowed. He's *definitely* going to strike you down now. It's a shame. I was just starting to appreciate your company." No man could be struck down for falling for Caitlyn.

It's time to leave. I let go of her fingers, reluctantly. We gather our things and decide to get coffee. Caitlyn's only been in my life a few days and I already know more about her than any other woman I've met.

It has taken me by surprise. This constant attraction, every move she makes, every touch sending shockwaves to my groin. The desire to hold her hand, let her know I care. An overwhelming desire within me to protect and comfort her, above anything else.

Chapter Thirteen

Caitlyn

I peer out at the green fields surrounding us. Summer is approaching fast, but in the Hamptons, the weather is already glorious. Spring in London is several degrees lower than it is here, on average. It'll take a while to get used to the heat. At night, with the windows cracked open, I have the sea breeze to keep me cool, so reluctant to use the air-conditioning that everybody here loves so much.

I'd imagined living here for several years, investing in my work, but my contract is only for a year. Hank's intentions to walk away from the magazine as soon as he can are going to cut short my stay. I choose to ignore the fear that it will all come crumbling down and the fact that I can't get Hank out of my mind. It'll happen when it happens, might as well enjoy it while it lasts.

"I don't think I've ever been to a vineyard. Is it like a hop farm?"

He turns to me, inquisitive. "You don't have vineyards in the UK?"

It takes a lot of self-control not to roll my eyes at him. "You've been to the UK, right?"

"They have them in France. That's only a few miles away." The confusion on his face is charming.

"You're lucky you're handsome," I reply with a grin. To an American, even one as well-traveled as Hank, France is just down the road on the right from England. You could fit both the UK and France in Texas. It's all a matter of perspective.

"Are you calling me dumb?" He picks up the file I'd handed him when we got in the car and doesn't look up at me. It's not a joke. It sounds like it, he's smiling, vaguely but he's serious.

Hank is smart, book smart and everyday smart. He can make the perfect latté, fix a plug — fuck, he can even rewire a whole house — he can quote Shakespeare and Kerouac, but he has zero confidence in all that knowledge as if none of it is important. The desire to hug him and explain how much his knowledge is valuable overwhelms me, tell him that the people who think he doesn't matter because he didn't finish college or doesn't know all about the media industry don't count.

But they are the people who are supposed to be closest to him. His family. Their opinions *should* count the most. I wish I counted more in his eyes so that I could let him know his worth. He is priceless and unique and so very clever. I want to, but it would sound trite. I've known the man a week. He's hardly going to listen to me over the other people who love him.

I laugh. "Me? Never. I'm the epitome of tact."

"Not a word out of place," he replies, dismissively, without looking up from my notes about today's activity. "So what's so important that I gave up an afternoon of bathroom tiling?" I touched a nerve and I'm mad at myself for it.

"I don't think you're dumb." I blurt it out, putting my hand over the file he's reading, pushing it down so that he gives me his attention. It's silly, childish, but I can't bear the thought that he's angry with me.

He tips his head, chuckles to himself. Lifting my hand off of the file, he laces his fingers through it, placing them between us, his knuckles grazing my thigh. "I know."

It's getting complicated, this little game we're playing—brushing my shoulders whenever he passes my desk in the office, stealing each other's coffee as we're doing the morning briefing. It's like we're trying to convince ourselves that this is our new normal. I can't have you, but I claim you anyway. I'm going to just lay my hand in yours and pretend that this is completely acceptable, platonic behavior. It's not. It's physically and emotionally frustrating, and our bubble is going to pop.

He puts down the file and picks up his phone, one-handedly searching something about granite worktops. Hank's commitment to getting his house finished and sold is admirable. He spends every waking hour, when he isn't in the office or preparing Chad and Becky's wedding, working on the renovations.

But word has spread to local businesses about the magazine and I can't keep up with everything on my own. Today we're off to enjoy the perks of the job with our very own driver, courtesy of Baresi Corp.

The car draws up in a very stately courtyard. The winery itself is an architectural masterpiece and the vineyard surrounding it is just stunning — rows and rows of vines, with the sea as a backdrop. I take back my hand and ready my camera. This is cover-photo worthy.

"Mr. and Mrs. Walsh?" A very smartly dressed woman with a clipboard welcomes us at the front door. Hank and I look at each other.

"I didn't expect you to take my name, but that's very flattering, considering," I say. *Considering that yours got us the invite in the first place.*

He blushes. "We're uh— We're not together. Caitlyn Walsh, Hank Baresi." He holds out a hand and shakes hers. With the look on her face, it's a wonder she doesn't curtsey.

It had been explained to me that there are specific reasons as to why they hadn't hired a journalist from the US to work with Hank and I'm slowly starting to understand. He's fricking royalty on this island, one of the princes of this realm. I chuckle to myself, thinking about my grandmother and how she would have laughed. My heart pinches. I haven't yet mourned her. I pull myself together. I'm not going to do this now.

I pick at the fluff on my blouse and straighten my skirt. The woman and I are dressed almost identically, but my clothes are a size too small and I'm filling them with rather less grace than the person facing me.

She leads us through to an entrance hall. Hank turns to let me go first, placing a gentle hand on my back. My insides do a backflip. Prince Charming.

Inside it's beautiful, very Moroccan in style, plastered walls, colorful tiling. Nothing like anything

I've seen yet in my visits. I take the opportunity to start snapping away.

The quality of the workmanship is impressive. I let out a quiet little giggle. Hank's influence on me is showing. I'll be complimenting the condition of their grouting next.

Our guide, rattled by Hank's presence, can hardly speak. "Mr. Uh, Mr. Baresi…"

"Oh please, call me Enrico." I swear he rolled that R. Is he flirting with her?

A little tinge of green surges up inside me. I am not okay with that. I have no ownership of this man. Why then do I hate this so much? Have I staked my claim? One kiss and a couple of cheeky conversations, if we don't count what he doesn't remember, and I have decided that he is mine.

"Enrico. Ms. Walsh…" If she's waiting for me to say 'Call me Caitlyn' we'll be here a while. My hackles are up. "My name is Caroline. Please follow me. We're going to start with a tour of the cellars and then we'll move out onto the terrace for a tasting."

We follow her down a set of winding stairs to their perfectly chilled underground cellar. I shake my blouse, relieved to escape the heat. A storm is brewing both inside and out.

Caroline drones on about casks and aging, and I take photos and make notes. Hank just smiles flirtatiously and makes cheeky remarks about pumping and popping corks.

There's only one thing that I hate about myself more than my big mouth and that is my jealous side. It doesn't manifest like it would with, say, Becky, sharp-tongued or bitter. Quite the contrary, jealousy is the only thing that shuts me right up. I steam and boil inside like a kettle. I'm a sulker. It's a detestable trait.

"Well, that's everything to do with the winemaking process, now on to the fun part." We move out onto a terrace, climbing back up the stairs. This time Hank's hand is on her back as we reach the top of the stairs.

"Ladies first," he says, like a broken chivalrous record. I glance over and raise my eyebrows. He flashes me the perfect smile and lifts his eyebrows in reply. Am I missing something here?

The sky has darkened and the air is thick. The heat has reached suffocation point, especially after the chill of the cellar. Warm droplets of sweat run down my back and I pull at my blouse in an attempt to disguise it. It's too tight and is sticking to me, revealing the trace of my bra underneath. As sexy as it might sound, a sweat-stained blouse is not a good look on me.

Caroline is still perfectly coiffed, but my hair is rising like uncooked bread. "Ooh, it's so hot out here." I put my hand to my chest. "Any chance of doing this somewhere with air-conditioning?" I have cracked. I am American now. Air-conditioning has won me over.

She flutters her eyelids, taking in the sodden mess in front of her. "Oh, I'm sorry. You're not from here, are you? Mr. Baresi, Enrico and I...we're used to it." She places a hand on his arm, rubbing it up and down, getting a good feel, a solid grip.

Holy shit. Whatever happened to female solidarity? I've never punched a woman, but I'm close. I ball my fists, my nails digging into my palms. "Fine."

"Don't worry, Caitlyn, a couple of glasses of rosé and we'll soon be chilled right down," says Hank. He's still smiling at me. Is that a hint in some way? If he thinks I am going to stick around while he chats up this woman, he is sorely mistaken.

But I am, aren't I? We're not on a date here. We're working. At least I'll be getting free wine out of the experience.

Caroline takes us over to an outdoor bar, serves us each a glass of a dry white chardonnay and sets out a plate of savory crackers. "Before you drink, just take a second to smell the distinctively strong aroma and tell me if you can capture the fruity essence of this particular wine."

I'm no good at this, despite my Gallic next-door neighbors. "Blackberries?"

She turns toward Hank and laughs with such frivolity you'd think I'd just suggested it tasted like poop and unicorns.

"Enrico?" she says, placing her hand on his arm again as if he's going to run away. "I'm sure you're very knowledgeable about wine, among other things."

He grins back at her. "Oh, I wouldn't say that." Placing the glass to his face, his nose almost touching the wine, he breathes it in then pulls the glass away, holding his breath, contemplating. "Peach," he proclaims, sure of himself, releasing a long slow breath as he says it. I feel my eyes roll back into my head. Really? I'm right here, dude.

The way he says it, pausing for just a second to allow us to admire him, gets Caroline so flustered that I can hear her ovaries exploding from over here. "Yes," she whispers, composing herself. She turns in my direction. "Nice to see we have at least one connoisseur among us."

That's it. I'm going to drown her in her own fucking vat. Death by rosé. Not the worst way to go, admittedly.

"Oh, Caroline, you flatter me. It was just a guess." He runs a hand through his dark curls, and I swear Caroline whimpers.

Get a room already.

Without any seating at the bar, I have to stand through five more episodes of their burgeoning love story, each one steamier than the one preceding. While I, only a few feet away, slowly morph into a molten lump of sweat and hair. Slouching against the bar, slightly tipsy from finishing Hank's glasses when I've drunk my own, dehydrated from the sweating and crackers and fanning myself with my notepad, I come to the dawning conclusion that Caroline had won this round.

She can have him. Now, if they would just let me leave so I can die with dignity, this will all be over and they can go do it behind the barrels in the cold, cold cellar. I get excited thinking about it—the cellar, not them doing it. I'd sell a kidney for a bucket of ice right now.

"And it might surprise you to know that the last glass of wine was the same as the first. Your palette having adapted and changed throughout the tasting made you experience it in a very different way."

"Good God, really? No. That is shocking. Well, I think our car should be arriving shortly. Shall we take our leave, Enrrrico?" I can roll my fucking R's too.

"You won't be ordering today?" Caroline looks positively shocked. This is a visit for a news article, not a buying session. I look over to Hank. Ah, of course. He's getting his wallet out.

"That depends entirely on the terms. As a *connoisseur*, I do appreciate a good price for a good bottle of wine."

What is he doing? The storm is looming over us, and my body simply cannot take much more of this heat. "Well, I'll let you two negotiate." I place a clammy hand on Hank's incredibly dry shirt sleeve. The man is a mythical beast. "You can find me in the car."

I storm off...the wrong way. Do a walk of shame past them and head toward the car. Never has a woman been so grateful for air-conditioning. I lay my body down on that car seat and soak in all that refreshingly cold air. *Better than sex.*

It takes twenty long minutes before Hank joins me — twenty minutes where I go from angry enough to break something to just plain old sad and miserable.

What a stupid, ridiculous fool I've been, falling for his charm. He isn't my cowboy. He's a rattlesnake. As if I even had a chance with him. Thank God I hadn't slept with him. This's why I'd promised myself not to get involved. No more Mr. Wrongs, remember? When will I learn? The cold air is cooling my desire to ravage my boss. Good.

"Hey." He opens the car door. Looking like he's just stepped out of a magazine photo shoot, a bead of glistening sweat on his forehead the only sign of the fact that it is a hundred degrees out there.

"Hey." I don't look at him.

"I got us a great deal, twenty-five percent off. I ordered several different types. You can mix and match, whatever you want. Just a small thank you for all the work you're doing." That's a silver lining, at least. I have spent a rotten afternoon. A bottle of wine or two might make it better.

"Did you get her number too?" I try not to sound catty, but it's stronger than me.

"Who, Caroline? She gave me her card, yeah."

"Good for you." I continue to stare pointedly out of the window as the car pulls away. "It was all worth it then."

"Did you get everything you needed for your article?" He isn't getting the message that I do not want to talk to him.

"Yeah." I should write about how friendly the staff are.

We sink into silence. I sit back and look at my hands. Suddenly I miss the feeling of his hand in mine. I trace a heart shape into my palm, round and round. I'd thought maybe it was the start of something. I was wrong.

But it is too much to bear, the silence, the niggling jealousy. "So are you going to call her?"

"Who? Caroline. Why would I want to call Caro...ooh." He grins. "Did you think I was trying to ask her out?"

That's it. The little chuckle that emanates from his throat, the pity, it tips me over to the third and final stage of grieving a crush. Ugly crying. "You think this is funny?"

My stupid little weak heart is breaking, and he's looking at me like I've made it all up in my mind. I never learn. My tears are as much for me as they are for this relationship I've created in my imagination.

"No." He places a hand on my knee. "No, I thought it was funny that you thought I was flirting with Caroline in front of you. Oh shit, I'm sorry."

I purse my lips and nod. Yep. It isn't just a dick move. It is also not the first time someone has done that to me. "So? You never answered my question."

"No. I'm not going to call Caroline. I didn't even realize I was being *that* flirty. Yeah, I let her do her spiel, but I just thought it was to get us to buy more wine."

"Well, you were." The tears are really flowing now. What's left of my mascara must be running down my face. I run the back of my hand across my cheeks.

He reaches his warm, strong hand under my chin. Descending his soft, warm lips on mine. It takes me by surprise, then I sink into it and allow him in.

He pulls back, still holding my face inches from his. "I'm so sorry. I was thoughtless. I'm no good at taking it slowly." He hesitates. "That's what we're doing, right? It's not just me?"

I nod as best I can with his hand under my chin. "I guess. I don't know, are we?"

"I'm no good at this whole relationship thing. I just wanted to surprise you with a few bottles of wine." He pauses and bites his lip. "I want *you*, Caitlyn. I want to get to know you. I would never do anything to jeopardize that. It won't happen again. I promise."

He kisses me, his lips lingering long and hard on mine while his tongue seeks refuge within. I'm savoring every second.

I'm so conflicted, running hot and cold with him, this perpetual state of unknowing—wanting what I can't have, exhilarated by every touch and yet knowing that this is a dangerous road we're heading down.

"Hank, we shouldn't. We decided it was a bad idea," I whisper, convincing nobody. I look down at those soft, delicious lips, enticing me back onto them just by existing. "We shouldn't." If I say it enough times, it will be true.

"I know," he replies, licking his lips, likely memorizing the taste of my mouth on his. "I know."

Chapter Fourteen

Caitlyn

A ferocious wind almost blows me over as I step out of the car. The storm is coming in from the sea. "We should get the plants inside, just in case," says Hank, jumping out of the car, grabbing my camera equipment and heading toward the apartment.

We open the door, bring everything in. Only the sign remains over the porch, swinging violently to and fro as the wind bashes against it.

"Will you be okay?" he asks, looking out of the window.

"I'm a big girl."

"I know." He turns to me with a reassuring smile. "I'd rather stay until it's calmed down. The electricity here tends to be a bit temperamental. I'll cook us some food."

There is so much between us constantly being unsaid, pins in things, Post-it Note reminders for a later date. Maybe it's the ions in the air, charging up for the storm, but every hair on my body stands on end, static electricity surging through me. Anticipation.

"I never say no to food." We lock the door and head upstairs. I'm thankful for a brick building, not imagining how the wind must howl around Hank's wooden home. "But first I need a shower." A very cold shower to rinse that sexual tension right off.

Twenty minutes later, every last drop of sweat has been washed from my skin. Even my hair had been tamed into submission. I wander out into the apartment, wearing only my robe. "Do you cook?" asks Hank, rifling through my fridge.

"I left home at eighteen. I cook enough not to die of starvation. I wouldn't say I'm a cordon bleu." I grab a pair of lace panties from the drawer and slip them on.

"We could make tacos." It isn't a suggestion. He's already heaving flour and other ingredients out of a cupboard and emptying my fridge of chicken and peppers.

There's something incredibly sexual about a man preparing food. Hank, to all intents and purposes, had not come across as a man in charge of his life when he was lying on the floor of that bathroom trying to find a condom. But if you stick a hammer in his hand or watch him peel an onion, he is pure temptation. My stomach muscles jerk as I remember his fingers tracing the line of my stomach down to my crotch.

Breathe.

He begins to knead the dough. *Holy fuck, man. Have a little decency.* I steady myself against the kitchen island and fall down onto a stool.

"Tell me about your travels. Is that where you learned to do all this?" It certainly wasn't in his parents' home, with their full-time chef.

"I went to Europe, started in the UK and then moved across from France to Italy to Greece. I only saw the north of Africa, Tunisia, Morocco. I'm going to go back one day, see Kenya, Madagascar, the south. This has to rest for ten minutes. Shall we have a drink?"

Jen has stocked the fridge for me, including a selection of wines. For a huge American corporation, the Baresi family sure do look after their employees. He serves me a glass of wine — might as well go on as I've started — grabs a beer for himself then sits opposite me.

"And you?"

"I've been to France and Spain. Not very exciting. This is the farthest I've ever been from home." It's not the opportunity to travel which has restricted my travels, but my work ethic. I don't regret all the years spent working up to where I am now, just the lack of time for myself. I envy Hank's lackadaisical attitude to life. He takes me out of my comfort zone.

"Where would you like to go?"

I bite my lip. Replying '*to bed with you*' might be a bit forward for six-thirty on a workday evening.

"Am I going with you? I hear your plane etiquette isn't up to scratch."

"You're funny." He grins at me and sips his beer. The man looks like an advert for cold beverages on a hot day. My insides tremble and I catch my breath so he won't hear the quiver as I exhale.

"Do you not remember anything about the flight? Everything that happened before you streaked down the aisle?"

"A gentleman never kisses and tells." Does he know, does he remember? "No, I'm kidding, my brother gave me some kind of pill, supposedly to help me sleep, and I was totally out of it. I didn't even remember where I'd gotten the hat until some guy came over to ask for it back."

The wanton, frantic kissing in the corridor, the fumbling in the bathroom? Only I was witness to it. The unfinished business. I need him to feel that too.

"You were in the bathroom. You made a heck of a lot of noise. The woman next to me complained about it." I try to jolt his memory. "You weren't alone."

"Yeah, I woke up on the toilet. Scared the shit out of me, didn't know where I was. I think…" He hesitates like he's deciding whether to share. "I think you're right. I was in the bathroom with someone else, a woman."

"A woman?" *Me. You mean me. You were this close to fucking me.* I wave internally. "Do you remember anything about her?" He raises his eyebrows. I guess it is a strange question. "I'm just curious."

"It's just a feeling I have. I can't quite put my finger on it, like when you go into a room and you can't remember what you went in there for." He thinks about it for a second, takes another sip, looks deep into my eyes as if he's searching for the true inside me. "Nope, I got nothing." *Fuck.*

"Did they ever find your phone?" I cringe inside. I am never not going to feel bad about that.

"No. I had it backed up, so nothing was lost except my dignity and my Toon Blast score." Phew. "Shall we chop up some food?"

By 'we' he means him. I sit on my stool, legs crossed, glass in hand and watch him slice and dice the chicken and the vegetables, as he explains how he learned to make tortillas.

There is something very comfortable about our interactions. I'm no longer on the defensive. He's a natural charmer and has perfected the art of putting people at ease. The urge to stand up and slide between him and the chopping board is overwhelming me — to kiss his neck, nuzzle against that perfectly toned chest and feel the warmth of his body against mine.

I've already tasted this man too many times. I want more.

"I'm not being very helpful, am I?"

"I don't mind. This is nice." He smiles at me again and my vagina melts into a puddle of lust.

I open my mouth to confess something, but my brain steps in. We've only just got back on steady footing. Is it really the best idea to reduce his first memories of me to *almost-fucking in a plane bathroom*? Is that how I want him to see me?

I stand up to get the wine from the fridge and he turns to wash his hands at the same time. Inches apart, we once again find ourselves in a compromising position.

"Another beer?" The words come out strangled. I'm holding my tongue to stop it from entering this man's mouth.

He breathes. Deeply. Is his resolve waning too? "Please."

I shimmy past him, open the fridge and bend down to get him a beer. As I stand back up I can feel him behind me, so close that the warmth of his body sends a shiver down my spine. He reaches around me.

My mind flashes back to that night, his hand in my underwear, holding him up. I'm as turned on right now as I was in that bathroom.

He grabs the beer out of my hand. "Thanks."

A flash of lightning and simultaneous thunder crashes down outside and everything goes black.

"Shit." I jump back against him and he is once again holding me up. Why do I constantly swoon against this man? "I am so sorry. I really need to stop falling into your arms like this. We are not in a romantic comedy and I am *not* Meg Ryan."

"You kind of are," he replies, laughing and pushing me back up onto my feet. "I can see it. Are you a fan of those kinds of movies?"

"Oh my God, I hate rom-coms."

"You hate rom-coms? How can you hate romantic movies? I thought all women loved them." He lights the gas on the cooker hob and sprinkles a little olive oil into a pan.

"I came to the realization one day that everybody in rom-coms is inherently evil. Do we have any candles?" I rifle through the cupboards.

"Oh-kay. Why?" He opens a drawer and hands me candles and matches.

"Thank you. In *Sleepless in Seattle*, she strings along her fiancé while writing to another man, she hires a private eye to spy on that man and she dumps her fiancé on Valentine's Day."

I grab a small plate, tip a lit candle to get some warm wax on it and smoosh the candle down to secure it.

"To All The Boys I've Loved Before." Hank's knowledge of rom-coms is impressive.

"The one where she can't decide between him and several other guys or the one where she can't decide between him and one other guy…who she kisses?"

"Somebody hurt you bad in a previous life, didn't they?" It is said in humor, but it strikes a chord.

"All of them." That hurts as much to say it as when it actually happened. "It's possible that my heart has turned to ice, yes. As I said before, my love life had always been somewhat complicated." *Like right now in this kitchen.*

"You can't have given up hope. Don't you want to meet Tom Hanks and live happily ever after?" He flips his tortillas.

"It doesn't work like that."

"Why not?" *Because I've met the perfect man and I'm not even allowed to sleep with him and now every other man I meet will not even compare to you.*

"I think I'm just destined to be alone."

He wraps his arm around my waist, spinning me around holding me to him. "Nobody should be alone." He kisses me, his body relaxing against mine. We both release the tension that has been building since we stepped out of the car. We open up to each other.

He switches off the gas, one arm still wrapped around me, lifts me off my feet and carries me over to the bed. *Fuck.* It's the most impressive, slick move a man has ever made on me and my whole body applauds.

Lying over me, he pulls my robe open just a touch and slowly swirls his tongue around my breast.

"Wait." I fucking hate myself, but I can't do it. I can't let him go on without telling him the truth.

"What? Shit, if this is no, just say no. Caitlyn, you're killing me."

"No. I mean, no, it's not no. I need to tell you something." I kiss him, just a peck, then another, enough to reassure him that he has done nothing wrong. I scoot up the bed, and he follows, crawling up over me. My pussy is screaming at me to shut up, but my brain has way more morals than that part of my body ever did.

"On the plane." He nods. I'm pretty sure at this point he's just worried that I've seen his dick in Business Class. I could just leave it at that, say nothing and let him do his thing, keep this secret inside me forever. But there are a lot of secrets inside me, Post-it notes littered about my brain, and I desperately need to remove some of them so I can see clearly.

"Yes."

"It was me. We almost fucked." His eyes widen. It's done, I've done it. I hope to God it doesn't change anything.

"What?" He falls down beside me, excited confusion in his eyes. "What? When?"

"The woman in the bathroom. That was me."

"You? What?" Any fear I've had about telling him has dissipated. He's intrigued, but he doesn't look angry. He traces his finger along my stomach, rises and circles my breast. "I'm sure I would remember this body, these beautiful breasts." He flicks my nipple, sending a jolt through me.

"Yeah, uh, that's why I called you cowboy the first — well, second — time we met."

"And we... What did we do? Why didn't you tell me? You've kept this secret for like a week. It must have been killing you."

Why didn't I tell my billionaire boss about our drunken naked shenanigans? Gosh, I can't think.

"I have died inside many, many times. We did some stuff, a little kissing, a little under the clothes stuff." I squirm with pleasure at the memory of his hand on my clit. It's going to happen again. Oh my God. "I didn't know how to tell you."

"Fuck. I didn't... I wasn't inappropriate with you, was I?" I shake my head. Not in any way that I didn't want him to be. My heart flutters, like a chunk of ice falling off into the ocean. I peck him on the lips again, just to thank him for *that* being the first thought that entered his mind.

"No, no, not at all, the perfect gentleman, well, you know, it wasn't exactly gentlemanly behavior that I wanted, but don't worry. I was totally on board."

"Fuck. I am so sorry. I don't remember at all. Was I any good?"

I laugh. Is that his only concern? "You were great, for someone with very little hand-eye coordination." I have to stop and breathe for a second. I'm so hot for him right now. "But you were off your head and it didn't seem right to take advantage."

"So we never actually…"

"No. Like I said, it wouldn't have been right."

"And now?" He rips open my robe fully and takes in my body beneath him.

"We have unfinished business, Mr. Baresi." I unbutton his trousers. "Tell me you at least bought some condoms in the last week." His eyes widen. He's thinking about it.

Fuck, Hank. You have to be kidding me.

"No. But I know where there's a stash." He slides off of the bed, lifts the mattress and removes a box of condoms.

"I don't even want to know why you know that they're there." I pull him back up over me.

He sinks down onto me, nipping and biting at my body, making me wait for him when I've already waited so long. He drops his hands on to my shoulders. He slips his fingers under my robe and pushes it off me. He slides them down my body to my pussy, which is already wet for him. I've been waiting to relive this moment, and it is everything I remembered.

Once again, he sinks his hand between my legs. He slides his fingers under my lacy gusset, shivering with anticipation as he does it.

The familiar touch of his fingers on my pussy. "Tell me what you like," he murmurs in my ear as his fingers enter me, circling my clit with his thumb. Sober Hank is a gentle lover.

"This. Don't stop." I'm close, too close. I've been edging for a week now. I need to come. My body shakes as the waves of the orgasm rise up inside me. His mouth is on mine, catching my gasp. He lets me finish, slowly sinking down and removing my panties, leaving me fully exposed for him.

He drops his down between my legs, circling my clit with his lips. I jerk back. It's too soon, too sensitive, but he is hungry for me.

"Wait…"

He looks up at me from between my thighs. "I should have started with my mouth, huh? I didn't know how ready you were for me. I wanted to take my time."

I stick my hands into the curls on his head, tug on them hard enough to make him bite his lip. "You've been fluffing me for a week now. I'm ready."

He pulls away, sitting on his knees in front of me, and I get my first full view of his erect cock. *Bloody hell.* It's as impressive as every fantasy I've had since I'd seen it waved in front of my face.

He catches my wide-eyed regard. "What?"

"Your cock," I reply, looking up at him. It's such a cliché, but it is *huge.* I've felt it up, seen it whirling around in Business Class, but I've never seen it in action.

He winks at me and grins. "It doesn't just look good. It does stuff too."

Fucking Hank Baresi really will be every fantasy I've had come true. The man is a god, carved by angels.

"Uh-huh." I grab it, toy with it, slide my thumb around it, savoring the beauty of the beast. *Jesus, this thing is perfection.*

He slides my hand off, laughing. "Don't. It's been too long for me too."

I sit up, lean forward and swirl my tongue around the tip. "So I can't do this?"

"No." He gasps and pulls away from me, grabbing a condom and rolling it on.

He leans over me then pushes me onto my back with a gentle nudge. "You need to behave."

"You going to make me?" He kisses me again, separating my legs with his, preparing me.

His face takes on a more serious tone. "You sure you want to do this?"

I nod, as my body tenses in anticipation. I've never been so sure of anything in my life. He teases, entering slowly, breaking me in before filling me whole.

"Fuck." My mind detaches from my body. I close my eyes and try to concentrate on sensing every thrust.

He gasps with every movement, kissing me forcefully, his mouth hardly leaving mine. He is holding back, slowing his rhythm, doing his best to make it last. It must be killing him.

I grab on to his back. We're synchronized, writhing and twisting. He slows down, then stops.

He pulls out, lowering his mouth down to my pussy once more. He flicks his tongue at my clit, building me again.

I know he wants to make it last, but I want him inside me. "Fuck me," I whisper and he sits back and just admires me before rolling me onto my stomach and lifting my hips to glide back into me. His moves are slow and calculated. He slides his hand down. He circles my clit with his fingers.

"Come for me again," he says. I do his bidding because it is everything I want, and it is beyond my control. He has me, completely, body and soul. I am his.

As the storm rains down outside, the lightning casting shadows of our naked bodies on the walls, he brings me to orgasm a second time and we come gloriously, loudly together.

It is everything I had imagined. And so much more.

Chapter Fifteen

Hank

"I'm starving," I say as I hold Caitlyn to my chest.

It isn't a complaint as much as it is a statement of fact. The storm has abated, as have our ardors. We are both coming out of our post-sex haze and I am famished.

We've finally done it. My subconscious has been trying to tell me something all week. Turns out she and I had, as she put it, unfinished business. That explains all the uncontrolled boners every time I was in her presence. I'll finally be able to stand up in public again.

"I'm pretty sure the electricity isn't going to come back on tonight. Would you like me to stay?" Code for *I can't be asked to drive home now and I'm pretty comfortable naked in this bed with you.*

"Of course" — she curls her finger around the tiny hairs on my chest — "on the condition that you finish those tacos."

"I should get dressed first. It's chilly in here." Open-plan looks amazing, but it is so difficult to keep warm. I should have gone for radiant floor heating.

She sinks her hand down and swirls it around my balls. "Spoilsport."

I peck her on the lips. She's so impressed by my cock. I don't need her to see what happens when it gets cold.

Pulling on my pants, I get back to work in the kitchen. Caitlyn is on her phone, scrolling through her social media.

I rack my brain, trying to find something, some memory of that bathroom, but I've got nothing. That whole plane trip is a vague, foggy memory. That pill Leo gave me was not your momma's Ambien.

It isn't that I don't believe Caitlyn. She had been on that plane and there's some serious chemistry going on between us. I know drunk me too well. An airplane bathroom hook-up with a stranger? Well, let's just say it wouldn't have been the first time.

That's some fully fledged destiny shit right there, though. Getting it on with the one person who could save any hope I had of getting this magazine off the ground, while getting my renovation business going too. It could have gone so horribly wrong.

"Can I ask you something?" She nods. "Why did you tell me?"

"About the plane? Because I didn't want you to suddenly remember in six months' time and think I was some weird stalker who lied to you."

"So you're a truthful, weird stalker."

She tilts her head. "Not entirely. I'm actually a princess from a long-forgotten land and I'm richer than most of your friends." She laughs and bites her lip.

I throw my hands to my face in fake shock. "You got me good. Here I was thinking you were just like everybody else, but you secretly wear a tiara in the bath and have a butler hidden in the closet." I put the spicy chicken in my tortillas, add my chopped vegetables and plate up. "Are we eating in bed?"

"Yeah, if you want." She puts down her phone. "That smells delicious."

"Catching up with your family?" I hand her a plate.

"Thank you. No, some friends. It's a good friend's birthday lunch. I was just commenting on their pictures." She takes a bite. "Oh my God, this is so good."

"Right? Do you miss them, your friends?"

"I haven't really had time to think about it yet. I don't have a big circle like you. A couple from uni, some from school."

Really? I find that difficult to believe. Everybody she's met since she got here loves her. Even Nonna seems to like her and that woman is damned hard to please.

"Do you want to watch a movie or something? I could get a laptop from downstairs, share some data."

"Yeah, why not? It's cozy here in the candlelight, under the covers."

"No rom-coms though, right?"

"I don't mind watching them. I just think we have to be clear on the fact that they all have terrible motives." She's the first woman I've ever met who has something against romance. Like, she wants romance in her life, but she hates it at the same time. I slide my arm around her butt, bring her closer to me and kiss the top of her head. Nobody's going to hurt her again.

"So if we were in a romantic comedy it wouldn't end well because we're good people?"

"The first time I met you, you were literally off of your head on drugs, and within minutes, you had your tongue down my throat and your hand in my pants. An event which, apparently, you don't even remember. Plus, we're probably going to lie to your entire family and hide whatever *this* is from everybody, even your friends."

"You give a good argument. So in rom-com theory, we get the Happy Ever After because we're terrible people. We're not lying to each other though, no more secrets."

"Right." She purses her lips. Why am I not convinced? "It helps that I, your weird stalker princess, am deeply in love with you, though." It feels like she's deflecting. For someone who talks constantly, there's a lot she's not saying.

"I knew you loved me. It's my tacos, isn't it?" She's kidding, though, right?

She laughs. "I'm joking. You should've seen your face. You went from laughing to sheer terror in five seconds flat." She licks her fingers and puts down her plate. "Really, you have nothing to worry about. I don't love you. Yet."

Yet. She's kidding around, sure, but there's emphasis in that little three-letter word.

"I do. I think the fact that you've accepted me, even though the glass slipper didn't fit over my big toe and I'm still a frog, is very kind." I take her hand, kiss the back of it. "Princess, I love you."

"I thought as much. They should make a movie about us, with songs and dancing rabbits."

I look into her eyes, her hand still in mine. "I love your mouth and its ability to function without the use of your brain." I kiss her as she harrumphs in reply.

"And I love the way your breasts peek out of the top of your unbuttoned shirt when you're sitting at your desk, nestled there, enticing me." I put my plate down and grab her nipple, tweaking it between my fingers as it hardens to my touch. "I love these soft, ripe titties and I love your little belly and the sweet taste of your pussy and the way you wrap your legs tightly around me when I'm fucking you."

"You're such a romantic."

"Says the woman with the supposed heart of ice. Oh, I get it. You're *that* princess." Caitlyn is far more sensitive than she gives herself credit for. She's wary, but her walls are easily broken down when she wants them to be.

"I told you I loved you, though." She puts her hand to her chest in fake indignation.

"You did. I guess you're melting."

She goes to get up, but I pull her back on to me. "You don't want to watch a movie?" she asks.

I glide my hands around her butt, sliding her over my hardened cock. "No, I want to fuck."

"I think we just established we're making love now, not fucking."

I laugh. Funny and dirty and hot as hell. This is the Caitlyn that only I see.

In front of my mother she's politeness incarnate, unassuming. With my friends she's professional, reserved, but with me she's a completely different person.

I stick my head between those titties and run my finger down to her core. She's my weird and wonderful stalker princess, who doesn't love me...yet.

Chapter Sixteen

Caitlyn

"I have no clothes. Nothing, I have nothing to wear. I'm going to have to go to your parents' house naked." I hold up a pair of panties and some very short shorts.

He snatches the panties out of my hand. "I like these. You should wear these so I can rip them off at some point."

"Give them back. That's my last clean pair." He dangles them over me, just out of reach.

"What's it worth?"

I scowl. "How about, when we're at tea with your parents I don't talk about what we did last night?"

"Caitlyn Walsh, you are a worthy adversary." He hands me the panties and snuggles up to my bare breasts. "Much as I would pay good money to see you strut your naked butt around my parents' house, I'm afraid we're going to have to come up with something slightly more decent for my mother's annual Saturday tea. What about the dress you wore to the baby shower?"

"Drycleaners."

"Would you let me buy you something?"

"You already bought me the shoes I wore to the baby shower." I try not to look too guilty. "Jen made me do it. She said it was company expenses."

"Not entirely foolish. I don't pay expenses, my father does. He can probably afford another couple of outfits. This is a workday, after all."

"I don't need you to do that. I can buy my own clothes. I'm really uncomfortable with this sort of thing." I shake my head in despair. Money isn't the problem, keeping up appearances is. "It's just a loan, until I get paid, agreed?" I'm digging a hole here. No more secrets, he'd said. I've never been part of Hank's plan and he hasn't been part of mine. Things have just gotten away from me.

"Agreed. Listen, you haven't met my father. Once you meet him, you won't regret a single penny you spent in his name. His utter dislike for you and everything you stand for will be enough to make you want to spend all the rest of it."

"He can't be that bad." Hearing a son talking about his father in that way shocks me. It isn't reassuring when even your boss's kids hate his guts.

"He is the head of one of the biggest media corporations in the world. So many people hate him that he has a security detail and an administrative department that deals entirely with death threats. And he is Nonna's son."

"Good point. I still feel bad though."

"Don't. You deserve all the beautiful things."

All right, flattery will get you *everywhere*.

"You're thinking about ripping that dress off me when we get home, aren't you?" He smirks, earning him a slap on the butt. "Dirty boy. I have to pick up the flowers I ordered for your mom."

"You don't have to keep doing that." He looks uncomfortable. It's bad enough that he is dating a pauper, but this pauper insists on buying bouquets for his mom. He doesn't have to say it. I've met enough Hamptons residents this week to know how things are. I'm 'them' and he is 'us'. It hangs over our relationship. And, just like my pile of dirty washing, the whole situation is going to have to be dealt with, eventually. Sooner rather than later.

* * * *

Mama Baresi is waiting for us at the door, just like last time. Her hair is down today. From a distance, she could be Jen's twin sister.

Once again, her arms are wide open and welcoming. "Enrico, Caitlyn."

"Mama, these are for you." I've gone for a different choice this time, lavender. "You mentioned last time we were here that you were having trouble sleeping, so I brought you these. If you dry them and put them under your pillow, they'll help you sleep."

His mother, delighted with her gift, leaves us to show the bouquet to her husband. We enter the house and admire the chaos, hesitant to know where to start. There are people everywhere, noisily talking over each other, dripping with expensive clothing and even more expensive jewelry. I'm so glad I didn't wear those short shorts.

"Do you know what breaks the most glasses at these gatherings? Italian arms. We can't tell a story without making it into an epic tale — *The fish was this big*, or *She told me she loved me*. It all has to be said with great gusto," says Hank, watching the crowd.

As he is talking, several small children notice us and come flying over, jumping into his arms. "Uncle Hank, Uncle Hank!"

"Careful, guys," says Hank, grabbing my arm as they nearly bowl us over

"Is she your girlfriend, Uncle Hank?" asks a cute little blonde girl.

He shakes his head. "No, just my friend."

"Chloe, Marco, Peter, leave uncle Hank alone. You can play with him outside after lunch. Mama has put out the bouncy castle for you."

An incredibly handsome man who looks just like Hank, but maybe five or six years older, shakes my hand, obviously one of the brothers. "Hi, I'm Antonio, Tony. Chloe and Marco are mine, as is Eddie, wherever he's got to. He's twelve and can't be torn away from his phone to talk to actual, real people."

"Bro. Looking handsome as usual," says Hank. I'm totally intrigued now. Do they all look as gorgeous as these two? His parents have some good genes.

They do a brotherly hug-type thing and I fiddle with my camera while they talk about the kids and school and Tony's wife, who is somewhere talking about their pool installation with one of the neighbors, apparently.

"Where are your other brothers?" I ask, scanning the crowd. "I want to meet Mario and Luigi." Hanks rolls his eyes.

I'd missed meeting Leo at the baby shower. He is one of the ones I am dying to speak to. His reputation precedes him. The sleazy one.

"Enzo's out by the pool," says Tony. He turns to me and leans in. "He doesn't like social situations. Don't be offended if he's not very talkative." There's an awkward pause. He excuses himself and goes off in search of his children.

"What's the story with Enzo?"

Hank fidgets, before replying, "Enzo, Lorenzo, he's my oldest brother. He lost his wife three years ago. We, uh, we've been trying to get him to talk to someone, a therapist, but he doesn't want to know. His kids live on campus. Erin's in Florida, I think. Josh is in Washington DC. He gets pretty lonely." He looks so sad. He's lost a sister and it shows.

"Oh, I'm so sorry. That's really sad." I am desperate to hug him, but I'm forbidden from touching him here. *Stupid rules.* I change the subject. "How about we go on through to the garden?"

"Not before we go to the kitchen. That's where all the gossiping happens at these things."

He's right. Jen and a couple of other young women are busy preparing pasta. They are covered in flour and are far more occupied with mucking around and making a mess than actual food preparation. Supervising them is my arch-nemesis and a woman who I dearly hope can smell the scent of Hank on me. Nonna.

Cigarette holder in one hand, drink in the other, she is true to form. "Thinner, no, not like that." From the disgusted look on her face, nobody in this room can even come close to making pasta like her.

"*Buongiorno*, Nonna," I say. She mutters something vulgar in Italian and smirks at me. Hank, bless his heart, chokes and coughs it out. He turns to me, desperation in his eyes. I know I'm supposed to shut up and put up. I'm not stupid. "Lovely to see you again too."

I plaster on the biggest smile. I'll save my knowledge of Italian for later. Making Nonna squirm when she finds out I know what she just called me will be priceless.

Jen laughs at her brother's reaction. "Anybody need me to translate?"

"Shut up, Jen," says Hank.

"Do you want to join us?" she asks, offering me a place next to her.

"No, thank you. We are supposed to be working today. Well, when I eventually convince my esteemed colleague here to stop enjoying the party so much."

"Duty calls." Hank dashes out of there as fast as his legs can carry him before his grandmother says anything else.

"She doesn't mean it," he says, as soon as we are out of earshot.

"Sure, she's a doll," I reply, letting the sarcasm drip from my mouth.

A gong clangs and the guests all shuffle outside. The buffet tea is to be served in a marquee in the garden. I'm expecting something impressive. This isn't my first Hamptons gathering, after all, but the amount of people, food and extravagance are all terribly overwhelming.

"This is just a spring tea party, right? You're not celebrating anything in particular?"

"I'm not going to have to remind you we're very, very rich, am I? It gets a bit embarrassing after a while." He shrugs. "I guess I just think of this as normal. I never really thought about how it looked to other people. What were tea parties like at your grandparents' home?"

"My grandmother wasn't very sociable."

"Wasn't?"

"The second funeral," I reply. I don't want to talk about that. He waits for me to continue, but lets it drop when I say nothing more. The loss of Gran was final, like the last link of the chain. My father is alive, but he has never been a parent to me. I am alone and until I grasp the reality of that, I can't even imagine trying to talk about it with someone else.

I fiddle with my camera again. I really need to start taking some photos, but when I look up, Hank is heading off toward a group seated near the pool.

"Guys, this is Caitlyn, my editor. This is Matt, and this here is Enzo. The oldest and youngest of my brothers." They stand up and shake my hand. The tall, handsome gene pool is incredibly strong in these men. If you lined up all the Baresi boys in front of me, you would just have a younger to older version of the same man. Enzo is a wrinklier, grayer version of Hank. It's uncanny.

"May I take your photo? It's for the magazine."

"Of course. Not with fuckwit though. He'll break the lens." Matt pushes Hank precariously close to the pool. He thinks he's hilarious.

"Matt, manners," says Enzo, smiling through gritted teeth. "Of course, where would you like us to stand?"

"What? Like you don't call him 'fuckwit' too." Hank says nothing in reply. Head bowed, tight-lipped and silent, his lack of confidence around these two is evident. The camaraderie here isn't the same as with his friends. There's a hierarchy being respected and Hank is at the bottom of it. Being the youngest of five brothers, he was probably the one who'd gotten his head farted on the most.

I don't recognize the cheeky, confident man I'm falling in love with and it bugs me. I resist the desire to grab his hand, to reassure him. If Matt is determined to be an asshole, I'm going to have some fun with him instead.

"So, Matt, you're the oldest of the brothers then, right? I know Hank's the youngest. Is there a big age difference between all of you?" I lean toward him, place my hand on his arm and ask him to bend forward for me. Hank crumples his eyebrows, confused, and I throw him a wink.

Without a word I reach into the bottom of my bag for my compact and tap the crown of his head with it "That's better. Gets rid of all that shine."

He isn't losing his hair at all. Quite the contrary, the Baresis all have a mop of curls, but he immediately throws his hand to his head. "Shine?"

I squeeze his arm. "Oh, I've embarrassed you. I'm *so* sorry. I mean look at Bruce Willis, bald as an eagle, still very popular with the ladies." I take my photos and Matt immediately excuses himself without another word to his brothers.

"Did I go too far?"

Enzo is laughing so hard that he's stuffed his serviette in his mouth and is trying to catch his breath.

Clearly not.

"Oh my, I don't think I've seen anything so funny in ages." He takes a deep breath. "The look on his face was priceless. You know he's only a couple of years older than Hank, right? I'm the oldest, by the way, then Leo, Tony, Jen and Matt and then Hank."

"Oh, she knows," adds Hank, a huge grin on his face.

We wander around the garden taking photos and writing down names. Mama has given me a list of contributors to her charities who must be included in any articles, without fail. I'm always happy to oblige. It is, after all, a Baresi Corp. magazine. Hank leaves me while I finish by getting a few candid shots of his family.

Once we've gotten enough photos to write an article longer than *War & Peace* I call it a day. I find Hank, who's at the bar with friends, and pull him aside. "I should go."

"Stay, have something to eat. I've booked a car. You can have a drink if you like." He places a gentle hand on my back and pulls me in close. He definitely gets the better end of the deal at every party we go to, free drinks every time. "Come on, princess. One drink won't hurt."

I'm sorely tempted, especially with that warm hand around my waist, but as the sober one here, I'm also going to have to be the sensible one. "I don't think that would be appropriate, Hank. I'm your employee, *remember?*"

He grabs my hand, but I pull it away, looking around us. "But you're so pretty in that dress and it's a lovely day. Nobody will mind." They will, especially his grandmother. I don't fancy having another chat with her about employer-employee boundaries.

Then, as if fate has decided to take a hand, Jen comes over to us, loops her arm through mine and drags me away. "Walk with me." She pulls me over next to Enzo and Tony and we watch as Hank's mother descends on him, a murderous scowl on her face.

"What's going on?" I ask, as Hank's mother screeches at her youngest son in Italian, her arms flailing, her voice getting higher and higher.

"I have no idea, but she's pissed." Jen grabs two glasses of champagne off a tray as a waiter passes us by. "Here you go. I don't know what Hank did this time, but it hasn't been this good since Matt borrowed Dad's Porsche and ended up in a ditch."

I put my glass on the table, to Enzo's surprise. "I'm working," I say with a smile. "In fact, I should really be leaving."

"I would if I were you. It looks like they're talking about you," says Jen. The hand gestures were indeed often pointed in my direction.

"My Italian is limited. What are they saying?"

"Uh, apparently it's been suggested that you've been working alone while Hank has been working on that house renovation in company time," replies Enzo. He winks at me conspiratorially.

"Oh thank God, I thought they'd found out we've been fuuhhck..." I forget myself for a moment, transfixed by this very public argument. So comfortable in these people's presence.

Three-sixths of the Baresi children turn to stare.

"What?" asks Jen, sticking her hand over her mouth as if in shock, when it's clear as day that there is a grin on her face as wide as the Cheshire cat's.

Tony and Enzo share an unsurprised look, shrug then flatter me with the international nod of fuck-partner approval.

"Sorry," I add. "I didn't mean to say that out loud." As usual, my *shut up* filter isn't on.

"Are you kidding? No apologies necessary. This is the best Saturday tea we've had in years," says Jen, putting a reassuring hand on my arm. "I just found Matt looking in the hallway mirror, trying to find a bald patch on the back of his head. I hear this is your doing."

"What did you tell him?" asks Enzo, starting to laugh again.

"I told him he'd been bald for years," she replies, proudly. Enzo laughs, loudly and with fervor. Tears stream down his face. He laughs so much, in fact, that he falls backward over a chair and just lies there, still chortling away, the whole party looking on. His mother stops yelling at her youngest son and turns to see what the fuss is about.

Hank runs over and helps his brother up. Enzo is bent over, holding his hand on his chest while he catches his breath.

Mama arrives, panicking. "Are you okay? You want some water?"

"Mama, I'm fine. I'm having a ball. Stop giving Hank a hard time. He's been working very hard on...*with* Caitlyn." He laughs at his own joke, then stops to pause for breath again. "Mama, Hank has never been to your Saturday tea. Enjoy the fact that he's here and that he is finally working, thanks to this lovely woman. Seriously, Hank, don't fuck it up. Getting Caitlyn to work *under* you is one of the best decisions you've ever made."

Hank looks at me and I shrug and whisper, "Sorry." I've told half of his family we're fucking. I'll have to make that up to him later.

Enzo gives me a wink, then he hugs his mom and she starts to cry and hug all of her children, exclaiming her love for them, loudly, in Italian.

Special events in the Hamptons might not be my cup of tea, but I can see myself learning to love the Baresi family parties.

Chapter Seventeen

Hank

"We have to be really careful," I say, "about the whole work situation."

"No, *you* have to be really careful. I haven't done anything wrong." The Monday-morning briefing with Caitlyn is chilly. She's been off-color since Saturday. Even my shoulder massage is coldly received, and that normally gets me a kiss on the hand and a contented sigh.

"You were the one who told everybody that we're fucking." Caitlyn and her unstoppable exterior thought process.

"And you got handsy at the bar, in front of everybody." *Shit. I did. She's right.* "We're young, healthy, single people. Nobody has been harmed in the joining of our pelvises. It's not like we're getting married and having babies."

"I'm supposed to be your boss." The Baresis don't cohort with employees. I've had that drilled into me since I was a teenager. I don't have to agree with it to know that my family will look badly upon it.

"You're the boss? You're never here."

"I'm here every morning."

"Last week you had a suit fitting for Chad's wedding on Wednesday morning and Friday you took two hours off for a haircut. Admittedly, that barber did things to your curls that makes my lady parts do somersaults, but that's not the point."

Oh yeah?

I grab her by the waist and spin her around. "What's *really* wrong here, princess?"

"I hate sneaking around like we've done something wrong."

I brush a curl from her face and look into those beautiful brown eyes. "But, you understand that it's complicated, right? I can't just admit it." I have too much to lose, her included. She gets that, right?

"Is it them you're afraid of losing or their money?"

I haven't really thought about it. Being cut off financially wouldn't be associated with being cut off emotionally. Mama would never do that. My father is another story entirely.

"Does it matter?"

She looks down at her hands. "Yes."

"Princess, you know how I feel about you and that I don't care about you not being like us. They don't feel the same, and they would make it very hard for us to be together. Have I ever made you feel like you were…less?"

"People in your family keep insisting on giving me clothes so I fit in, and it makes me really uncomfortable.

I can buy my own clothes, you know. And your mum went apeshit the other day about you working on the house."

"Buying you a dress doesn't make you a kept woman." I take her in my arms and kiss the top of her head. Cait is so precious to me and it hurts to make her feel like anything she's doing for me is wrong. "You have never asked me for anything. I know who you are. You make me feel like I count, and you don't look down on me because I didn't finish college or because I want to spend most of my life covered in dust with a hammer in my hand. I would never look down on you because you don't come from money."

"It's just that..." We're interrupted by a knock on the door. "This conversation is not over," says Caitlyn. Not one person has knocked on the door since we'd started this operation. We separate, move away from each other, just in case.

"Hello, anybody here?" Chad walks in swiftly, followed by a cameraman, a sound man and his producer.

"Chad, what can we do for you?" It's been a while since I've been featured on Chad's reality TV show. He's made it to five seasons. Only one more and maybe he'll get a movie.

"I haven't been here before. It's very..." He hesitates, searching for the word.

"Quaint?" says Caitlyn with a wry smile.

"Yeah. Quaint." He stands there, his hands in his pockets. We wait for him to speak.

"So," says Caitlyn, "what can we do for you, Chad?"

"You're a journalist, right?" She nods. "Have you done, you know, any investigative stuff. You know, tracing phones, following people?"

"You mean like a private investigator? Not really. I have done some research for different articles. What do you need to know?"

"I, uh, I think Becky is cheating on me." Caitlyn gives me the least subtle side-eye ever known. Fuck, she was right. I hate cheating. Despise it. Makes me so mad.

I reply with a look that says, *don't you dare open that mouth of yours*. She glances over at the cameraman, who promptly zooms in on Chad.

"Please try to avoid breaking the fourth wall," says the producer, handing us consent forms to sign. We sign, then we have to wait a second for everybody to get into position.

"Okay. And how do you think we can help you? And if we do find out that she's cheating, are you sure you really want to know?" asks Caitlyn. "Because once you know, you know that there's no going back. Trust me. You can't forget things like that. It changes everything, forever."

Chad perches on one of the desks. He pulls his fingers along his brow and rubs his eyes. This isn't the guy I know. Of the four of us, Chad is the archetypical billionaire's son. His dad paid him through college, he's an 'influencer' online and a reality star on cable.

The irony of companies sending their products to him for free when he is one of the richest among us is laughable. He might not always be respected for who he is, a product of his parents' money, but we all love him for his character. The life of the party, he's also a lost soul, kind and sweet and very loyal to us and Becky. A sheep in wolf's clothing.

"I don't know. Yes. We've been having…problems for a while now. I, uh, I might not have been entirely faithful myself."

What the fuck, you have to be kidding me. I refrain from saying anything. I look at my feet and stretch out my hands. I have this thing where I ball my fists up so tight that I cut my palms and I'm conscious that I'm doing it on camera.

"Okay. Where is she today?" asks Caitlyn, abruptly. She doesn't like a cheater. She's made that very clear.

"Right now? I don't know. She's got a final dress fitting with the girls this afternoon."

"Does she have Snap?" Both Chad and I look at Caitlyn as if she's just walked out of the middle ages. "Okay, so if she has Snap, you know you can find her location on it, right?"

Chad pulls his phone out of his back pocket.

"Give me your phone," I say. "I'll look if you like." He hands it over. Poor guy really doesn't want to know.

I tap on her name and search her location.

Ah. Fuck.

She's with Jonny. It doesn't mean that they're sleeping together. I've hung out with Becky and Claire in the past and I've not fucked either of them. But Caitlyn sensed it, and this only confirms what she thought.

"Where is she?" he asks.

I look over at Caitlyn and she just knows. *Shit. I don't want to tell him, but a part of me is so mad at Becky and Jonny right now. Especially Becky. Cheating with a guy who we all know will dump her when he gets bored with her.* He was even coming onto Caitlyn the other day at the party.

"We'll go with you," I say. This is a terrible idea, but it has to come out, right? Before they get married and it becomes a million times more complicated.

"We?" says Caitlyn, her eyebrows lifting in interrogation. "I have work to do."

Yes, we. I can't do this alone, I'm about to explode my whole friends group. "I would very much like it if you would come too." *I need you, you're my person.*

We take my car and Chad and his crew follow behind. Jonny doesn't live far. He too is a product of billionaire's row. His official profession is Competitive Sailor, but what that meant was apart from winning a couple of important races a few years back, he basically spends most of his life fucking hot strangers on his boat.

"You're so calm," says Caitlyn as she blots her face with a pink and beige ball.

If you only knew just how angry I am right now. "Why wouldn't I be calm? She's not my girlfriend. What are you doing?"

"Well, if I'm going to be on camera, I don't want to look like I only got four hours' sleep last night." She winks at me and rubs her hand up my thigh. "I meant that you don't seem fazed by the fact that one of your friends is sleeping with the other friend's fiancé and that that friend admitted to cheating on her. It's okay to be freaking out right about now." I'm normally so bad at hiding my emotions. I'm wound up like a fucking spring right now.

"Chad and Becky have a complicated relationship. I was with her before Chad, remember? She was supposed to be my prom date. Stood me up. There was a huge fuss and they kind of felt they had to make a go of it." It wasn't that she didn't want to be with me. It was the way they did it.

"Prom? No way." Caitlyn snaps her head round and smudges her lipstick. "I still think it's weird that Becky is making her way through the gang."

"No. Becky and I were kids. We didn't even sleep together, and this whole thing happening today is just a product of two people who were on a rocky patch and got engaged instead of splitting up."

"For someone who claims to have never been in one, you know a lot about relationships."

I know fuck all, but I've seen this a million times.

"I haven't spent the last twenty-eight years with my eyes closed. Look... I wouldn't hold it against Becky. You've seen what our parents are like when it comes to dating. She's got slim pickings if she wants to date someone with the same lifestyle as her. We're not like everybody else." We're a whole different species at times.

Caitlyn leans forward, right up close to the mirror, scrunches up her nose and draws a line along her eyebrow. "I guess you're right. So how many people have you slept with?"

"What?" I choke on the word and cough it out. Why does she need to know that?

"I need to know if I'm getting involved with a Chad or a Jonny, and your good looks and hot body are just blinding me from the truth."

"I'm not like them." *Trust me.*

"Well, then you won't mind telling me. I'll go first if you like...seven. Three long-term relationships and some teen romances."

"Seven?" Only seven? I'm fucked. Too fucked. Overfucked?

"Yeah. Is that a lot?" Nope. "Go on then. Tell me."

"Fortyish?" I haven't actually counted. I'm *well-traveled* as Ted puts it. Caitlyn doesn't reply. She just stares at me, her tiny brush waving in the air. "No more than fifty," I add, trying in some way to reassure her

She swallows loudly and looks down. "Protected?"

"Oh yeah, God yeah, never without protection. Wow. No. It's all good down there." She tips her head to one side, looked out of the window, avoiding me. "What are you thinking?"

"I'm wondering if I'm a notch on a bedpost." I guess I deserve that. I'm hardly looking good right now.

I place a hand on her thigh. "I can promise you, you're not."

Caitlyn isn't a fling. She's someone I want to get to know, to invest in. I haven't disrespected or used women in my past. I've just not stayed around long enough to make a connection. This is different.

We draw up in the harbor car park, get out and walk over to Chad's car.

"Are you sure you want to know this?" Caitlyn asks Chad, one last time. "Sometimes you find things out about your partner that you'd rather not have known."

Ouch. I'll be needing some cream for that burn.

This isn't how I want to spend the day with my girlfriend. It hasn't had an auspicious start and is steadily going downhill.

Jonny's boat is moored at Hampton Bays, among the million other yachts that rich people buy and never use.

Chad pales. "Isn't this... Is she with Jonny?" He chokes on the name.

"You wanted to know," I say. My heart breaks for him. He obviously wants to know the truth, but who the hell wants to know you've been banging someone who's been banging Jonny? My skin crawls just thinking about it.

It's only ten-thirty, but the sun is already blazing down. This has to be the hottest month of June in years. Hampton Bays is beautiful — the sea, the shiny white yachts clanking as they bob on the water. I'd have preferred to bring Caitlyn here in better circumstances.

Ted's car rips into the car park and parks next to mine. He jumps out, walks around the car, helps a very sweaty looking Claire to heave herself out of her seat and joins us.

"Aren't you supposed to be at work?" I ask. That guy is *always* at work.

"Early paternity leave. My wife needs me to dress her and rub her feet." He smiles at her, seeking some form of gratitude, but she's leaning against the car, waving a homemade paper fan under her armpits. Pregnancy does not look fun.

"What are you doing here?"

"Someone messaged us." I look over to Caitlyn, who shakes her head. "Said they needed moral support."

"I thought *everybody* in the situation might need someone." Chad has texted Claire so she'll be here for Becky. What the hell is going on?

Jen drives into the car park and parks next to Ted.

"What the hell? Who called my sister?" It's not bad enough that we're participating in Chad, Jonny and Becky's shitshow, now they had an audience too? I keep my mouth shut. *This is their mess, I guess.*

"Anybody want to tell us why we're here?" asks Ted.

Chad shakes his head. Fine. He's invited the whole damned gang, but I'm the one who has to explain why.

"We think Becky is having an affair with Jonny."

Jen and Claire pale, lips pinched. *They know. Of course they do.* Women talk about these things. I see my friends a couple of times a week and had no idea one was lying to the other one's face.

Caitlyn steps over toward me, her fingers play with mine, not quite holding my hand. My heart does a leap. "I should do it. I should go in there and tell them everybody is outside. Becky doesn't care for me and Jonny hardly knows me. I'm of no significance to them." This again.

"But you could be." She tips her head to one side. "I've never brought a girlfriend into the group, but if I did, I wouldn't want everybody to hate her. It has to be Chad."

"Okay, we need to put a pin in the girlfriend thing, because I adore you for saying that, despite the fact that I am super mad with you at the moment, for several reasons, but Chad is clearly not going to be the one to go in there. There are things you can't unsee." Her grip on my hand tightens. I lift her face to mine and kiss her. Fuck it if my friends see. I like having someone by my side. I don't care what they think.

"Okay. Chad, I'm going in." I start walking toward Jonny's boat before Chad can stop me. The cameraman follows me, but I turn and leer into the camera. "Fuck off."

I can hear Chad arguing behind me, the others holding him back. I just keep walking.

I hate boats. Rich people are supposed to love them, but the minute I get on one I start throwing up. The ferry from Marseille to Tunis was a killer, twenty-two hours on a boat. I nearly died.

I step onto Jonny's boat. My stomach flips. I can't tell if it's the boat or the fact that I'm about to interrupt my friends' coital acrobatics. "Hello? Anybody home?"

No reply. I knock and open the door. Please let them be playing Monopoly or chatting about how much Becky loves Chad.

Because karma hates me, they're naked wrestling. Loudly. The bedroom door is half-shut, and that isn't the sound of two innocent people doing a crossword.

"Guys. It's Hank." Fumbling and stumbling noises replace the ecstatic moans. I take a deep breath. I do not want to do this.

Jonny opens the door, naked as the day he was born, everything standing to attention. "Not now, Hank. I'm *busy*."

"Chad's outside. He wants to see Becky. And he probably wants to punch your face in."

Jonny steps back, looks over his shoulder then back at me. He lifts his hand to his face, covering his eyes. "What?"

Becky lets out a scream. Not an *I've seen a ghost* scream, more like the low howl of an injured wolf. She knows she is fucked. And I don't mean literally. Although...

"You probably want to get dressed. Everybody's outside."

"Everybody?" he asks.

"Yeah, uh, the whole gang's here—and a camera crew."

Jonny slams the door in my face. I can hear them muttering, their voices too low to understand. The only way off this boat is the deck or the deep blue sea. I know what I would choose, faced with my best friend or fiancé's wrath. But then, I can swim.

I step out onto the deck and heave. It's definitely the boat this time. Everybody is just standing there, waiting. Chad has his arms crossed, his face blank.

"Well?"

I shake my head. "Sorry, man."

"Okay." He turns to my sister. "It's over." She walks over to him, grabs hold of his hand. Oh, you have to be fucking kidding me. This isn't going to help persuade Caitlyn that we're not constantly swapping partners.

"What the hell is going on?" He needs to get his hands away from my sister.

"Remember when I said I may have had an affair. We, uh…" He pauses when he sees my face. "We may not have been entirely honest either." I am so disappointed in Jen right now, and a little disgusted.

Jonny and Becky walk out onto the deck hand in hand.

"Guys, we have something to announce," says Jonny.

"Jonny and I are in love." Becky looks into his eyes. I can see it now. I can see why Caitlyn knew.

Talking of Caitlyn, she looks as if her eyes are about to pop out of her head. It must all look pretty incestuous from her point of view. The bizarre world of billionaire's kids.

The cameraman pans the group to catch our reactions. Chad's producer isn't even trying to hide the grin on his face. This is TV gold.

The two couples size each other up.

"Jen," says Becky, "you're sleeping with Chad?"

"No. No." She shakes her head, blushing, but Chad nods furiously. He has no more fucks to give, except to my sister apparently. "Well, yeah. When you told me about Jonny, that you'd kissed him, my feelings for Chad began to change."

I heave again and I'm not even on the boat anymore. I don't want to know anything about my sister's love life.

"I think you guys need to all sit down and talk about this, get everything out in the open," I suggest. I'm not going to stand around the harbor all day because these idiots can't keep it in their pants. Caitlyn and I have work to do.

Ted and Claire walk back to the car with us.

"I was expecting a showdown, fireworks, shouting. I feel a bit let down now," says Caitlyn.

"Yeah it was a bit anti-climactic," replies Claire. "We'll have to watch the show to see if it got more heated after we left, and then there's the personal diary bits where they talk about what happened. We'll learn more then."

"You could just ask them," says Caitlyn, "seeing as they're your friends."

"Oh, we can't. They get gag orders, so they don't spill until you see it on screen." The things I've learned watching Chad's show... Drunken nights where my memory had been a bit fuzzy had come back loud and clear on the screen.

"Even to you guys?"

"Even to us," I reply, smiling at her.

"That's weird, right? You get that that's weird." She has a good point, but nothing in our lives has ever been straightforward and normal.

"Honestly," I reply, "that isn't the strangest thing I've ever seen."

We get back into the car and Caitlyn puts a hand on my arm and looks straight at me. "You know, you can talk to me about stuff. You don't have to bottle it up. It's not like I don't share everything with you." She does. The woman never stops talking. "It works both ways."

"My dad cheats on my mom. I found out when I was sixteen when I walked in on him and his mistress. I am forced to respect him because that's how my family works, but I hate him for how he treats her." My voice is choked, but I've cried enough tears for my mom over the years. "I hate him for it and I hate cheaters."

Caitlyn moves her hand up to the back of my head, plays with my hair. It soothes me. "I'm sorry. For your mom. That sucks. And for you."

"You've never done anything to make me doubt you, but you should know that I hate dishonesty. I won't stand for it." She balks a little. My voice is raised. I can feel her tensing up beside me. Deep breath. Caitlyn hasn't done anything wrong.

"Okay," she replies, quietly. "Noted."

She bows her head. Maybe I came on too strong. "Let's get back to work. I'll order in some food and you can show me the photos from this weekend." I flash my nicest smile at her. It's a little early in the relationship to be getting so angsty. I grab her hand, kiss it. "And then maybe we can take a little nap. It's been a long morning and we're both real tired."

Chapter Eighteen

Caitlyn

A week and a half I've been here. Only eleven or so days and in that time I've witnessed a summer's worth of drama amongst the inhabitants of this strange, exotic island. It's like a never-ending soap opera. Chad, Becky and Jonny's news rocked the community for about five minutes then everybody had decided that the wedding, having already been paid for, was still to be held. Jonny's parents would foot the bill instead of Chad's and we would never speak of this again.

And nobody thinks that this is strange.

As for Jen and Chad, they haven't been seen since. One hopes that the cameras aren't allowed into the bedroom too. Although, at this point, nothing would surprise me.

I might have done some online digging and found some clips of twenty-two-year-old Hank in season one.

Gave me quite a few cowboy flashbacks. Those were clearly wild times.

Hank has kept up his side of the bargain, watching the office in the morning and working on his house, discretely, in the afternoon.

Thus, today, as I chomp into a tuna sandwich and sip on my tea, he is already working on laying his flooring. I stare out of the window at the rolling ocean, reflecting on the complexities of life and a fleet of black cars with tinted windows draw up in front of the building. Crap.

I grab my phone. "Hank."

"Yes."

"I think your dad's here."

"Fuck." The sound of clanging tools resonates down the phone. "I'll be there in five minutes. Tell him I'm at lunch."

"Enrico?" Mr. Baresi is considerably shorter than his sons and portly in stature. He's also as bald as a coot except for five carefully greased strands of hair pulled from left to right over his head. Now I see why Matt was so stressed when he'd thought he was going bald.

He strides into the office, followed by a mean-looking security detail and several other people.

"Mr. Baresi." I gulp. We have never been formally introduced and I would have preferred it to stay that way. "What a lovely surprise. How can I help you?"

"Is he here?"

Shit. "He's out at the moment—lunch."

"Good. Take a seat." I half expect some kind of interrogation, a bright light, a case full of finger removal tools.

He sits at my desk and I grab a chair to sit opposite him. He is definitely the bad cop of the parents. "I've been hearing rumors."

"Rumors?" I can feel myself blushing. I'm English. That's what we do best.

"That Hank is working on the renovation when he should be here. And that the two of you are in a relationship."

"What? No." My brain has yet to engage. His beady little eyes bore into mine. He is, as many have already described him to be, a rather terrifying old man.

"Let me make it very clear that if any of these rumors turn out to be true, I will not only close down this magazine and Hank's little project, but I will also destroy you."

Destroy me? Are we talking in a professional capacity or cement shoes?

I sit back and look around at his entourage. None of them make eye contact. "Okay."

He smirks, his little thin lips trying their best to work their way into a smile, but they're so unused to it they can't quite make it. "I'm glad we're on the same page...uh..."

"Caitlyn." I have a sudden urge to take back control of the situation. "Would you like a coffee?" Even going to the kitchen five feet away had to be better than staring for one second longer into those bottomless pits of evil.

"Why not? Enrico insisted on paying for the most expensive machine on the market. We might as well use it. Karen." On a figurative click of his fingers, his assistant goes straight into the kitchen and starts setting up the machine.

Wow. He makes James Bond villains look positively sweet. His bodyguard doesn't have a bowler hat, but I don't fancy my chances nonetheless. I need to stay on his good side, but he needles me.

"I'll have a white coffee with two sugars," I say. Guillermo Baresi does *not* like this. His lip curls, and he lets out a tiny little growl. "I have the photographs from the tea party. Would you like to see? I took the opportunity to get some of your grandchildren."

"Why? Weren't you supposed to be concerning yourself with the donors to my wife's charity?" Ooh, snap. He's vicious.

"Oh, I got them too. More than enough for the article on both the website and the print version."

A couple of clicks on the mouse and the projector fires up. The late afternoon sun and the fact that the Baresi genes were of the flattering kind meant that I'd captured some amazing family photos. He sips his espresso and studies my work.

I don't know what I've expected of him. Hank has made it very clear that his father is a tyrant, both in and out of the office. Except, it appears, when it concerns certain members of his family.

He softens a touch at the photos of his wife and children. "You have an eye. Not bad for someone so young. Enzo's people were right to hire you."

"Thank you."

"You know..." — he waves his hand, struggling to find my name again — "honey, we're kind of a big deal over here. You keep on this path you'll go far. Anybody working with one of my sons needs to be objective, career focused. That wasn't the case with any of the people we interviewed for your position. You came highly recommended. I just hope your writing is as good as your photography."

Oh, it is.

"Where *is* that son of mine?" He looks over to the door as if that will make Hank arrive quicker so that he can stop having to talk to me.

"Yes, where is he?" *Good God. Get here before your father feeds me a poisoned apple.*

Speak of the devil and he will appear. Hank sweeps in, dressed far better than he probably had been twenty minutes ago. I scratch my head and give him a warning stare. Those curls capture all kinds of wood shavings and dust. He runs his fingers through his curly mop and sits down. "Papa, what an honor."

"I was just admiring the photographs from Mama's tea party. It was certainly worth investing in the better camera."

A camera is no good without a decent photographer, but hey, I've already got one compliment out of the man, I shouldn't expect miracles.

"Yes. So, what can we do for you, Papa?"

"Do I need a reason to visit my son?" Hank shakes his head and stands up straighter.

"No of course not, a pleasure to have you here." He rifles through the papers on my desk. "I have a hard copy of a series we're doing on churches in the Hamptons. Would you like to take a look?"

His father leans back in his chair, holds out his hand, into which Karen places his glasses, and he reads through the article, without a single word. I lean on the kitchen work surface, so nobody can see me trembling.

"Excellent work, son. You've done a great job. This is the quality of work we expected. Simple, clean articles about local life."

"It wasn't me. It was all Caitlyn's work. She's really the driving force behind this place."

Oh fuck. "No, I'm not!" What is Hank doing? Apart from the fact that he is looking at me with hearts in his eyes, he is also making it sound like I do all the work. "Honestly, *Enrico*, you should take more credit for your work."

He scrunches up his eyebrows. I can see his mind whirring, trying to work out why I'm not calling him Hank "Are you kidding me right now? Papa, since she arrived, she's written almost twenty articles, with photos, covering events, local business' everything we'd imagined for the magazine."

"Ha!" I laughed, theatrically. "You overestimate me, Enrico. I couldn't have done it without you." *Shut the fuck up.* I do not have any desire to find out what *I'll destroy you* means.

"Are you covering that farce of a wedding next week? I don't know what's got into your sister and that Ellisson boy."

"Enrico is in the wedding party," I said. "I'll be covering the event on my own."

His father turns and looks at me then turns back. "Do you want me to send someone along to stand in for you?"

"In the wedding or to work with Caitlyn? No thank you, Papa, Caitlyn is perfectly capable of covering it on her own."

"It's a big event." He leans forward and raises his voice a touch. "Important."

"I'm not sure I can do it without your guidance," I add.

Hank looks over to me and is near-fatally killed by the lasers shooting out of my eyes. "No. Thanks for the offer, Papa. We're good."

"Well, it's nice to see you have faith in your staff." With that he stands up to go, shaking his son's hand and striding out, followed by a trail of minions, without nary a goodbye.

I come out from my hiding place in the kitchen, walk over to double lock the front door and sit down at my desk. The seat is surprisingly warm, considering. "Well, I guess I've met your father now. He really loves me. I was thinking you and I could have a spring wedding."

"He doesn't actually like me very much either, if that's any comfort." Hank walks over to me, arms spread, and cradles me in them. It's my favorite place in the world to be.

I snuggle in, but I'm not quite feeling it. "He threatened me, us."

Hank freezes. "Threatened?"

"The *I will destroy you if you are sleeping with my son and letting him work on his restoration project* type of threatened. What does that mean anyway? Should I be leaving town? Changing my name?" Wouldn't be the first time.

"He hasn't had anybody bumped off as far as I know, yet."

"Yet?"

"He is Guillermo Baresi. We must all bow to his way. Leo's first and second wives were given sizeable checks in return for never speaking to Leo, and in the case of his second wife, their children, again. That's why this magazine was a means to an end. I only have to be a part of this until I finish my house, then I can walk away."

Walk away. Leave me to pick up the pieces, pack up my stuff and go, you mean. His callousness stings. "What happens to me? When you walk away and there's no Baresi running the place."

"You signed a twelve-month contract, Caitlyn." He waves his hands in despair. "Damn it. How could I have possibly known that I would have feelings for you, that you would be so invested in this project? You were supposed to just come in, set up the magazine and give me the time to finish the house."

"What are we going to do, then, when it's finished?" I don't want this over before it's begun. And by that, I mean the job *and* us.

"I have no idea. This is way too complicated, far more than it was ever supposed to be. I don't know what to do." He walks over to me and pulls me back into his arms. "I know I want to do it with you, though, however we make it work."

He kisses the top of my head and holds me to him. In the short time that I have known Hank, he's made a very lonely, lost girl feel loved and cared for. He's maladroit at times, but his sincerity shines through. I can't fault him for wanting to hide his job or our burgeoning relationship. Even we don't really know where we're heading. But the knowledge that our love—if that's what this is turning out to be—would carve a wedge between him and his family is devastating to me.

I've been alone for so long that the desire to belong is always hovering in the back of my mind. I've finally met someone who is the epitome of a family man and yet he will be forced to choose between them and me.

I'm so angry with myself. I have the power to change this, to be truthful with him, but I'm also angry with his family. It shouldn't matter. Caitlyn, the British journalist who loves their son, should be enough for them.

Sometimes, no matter how hard I try, I'm still a sad, broken child in a cold church, surrounded by strangers.

A rogue tear rolls down my cheek. "I think I need to go think about all of this." I head toward my apartment.

Hank grabs my hand. "No. You know how I feel about you, right? Please. You should have said something. He intimidates me everybody around him, but he shouldn't be intimidating you. It's not right. I won't stand for it." He took a deep breath. "Ever."

I curl up into his arms and raised my hands to his face. "This is so complicated." More than he can imagine.

"I'm not like them. I don't function like them. I'm sorry. You deserve better." He lowers his lips to mine, delicately brushing against them before taking all that anger and frustration out on my mouth. He lifts me off my feet and pushes me against the wall.

"Here?"

Unbuttoning my blouse with a mighty rip, he sinks his face into my breasts. "I want you now."

I drop to my knees and unzip his pants, releasing the beast. "How about I thank you for all the nice things you said about my work?" *Fuck*. It's all in my face, up close and personal. Lowering my mouth down onto him, I sink my hand between his legs and gently caress his balls.

Slowly, surely, I build him up, my hands and tongue reacting to every gasp that comes out of his mouth. He deserves this. He deserves every single sensual lick.

His ecstatic cries grow louder, releasing his resentment. He relaxes into me, his knees giving way. He pushes harder into me, wanting more, faster. "Hey." I pull back. "I'm in charge here."

"Sorry." He looks down at me and bites his lip as I lower my mouth back onto him, just the tip, my hands doing all the hard work. Leaning on the wall to steady himself, his head thrown back, he shakes and convulses as I bring him to fruition. I pull away and empty him over my breasts.

A blow job for my billionaire boss. So much for fighting the patriarchy. But Hank isn't the problem. He's trapped in a world he simply doesn't belong to. A world entirely controlled by his father.

I'm not mad at him, I'm not even mad at his family, except Guillermo fucking Baresi. I just can't see a way forward for us without somebody getting hurt. The more Hank and I fight to make it work, the more we fall for each other and the harder it will be when the truth comes out.

Dropping to his knees, Hank swirls a delicate finger under my chin and lifts my face to his. "How about we take the afternoon off? You've been working so hard and I need to make sure you are *thoroughly* thanked for everything you do around here."

"You're going to thank me personally?"

"I am going to thank you long and hard. I am going to thank you and then I'm going to thank you again and just when you think you can't take any more, I'm going to thank the hell out of you one last time."

Chapter Nineteen

Caitlyn

It isn't a bachelorette party, as such, more of a girl's night in, or so I've been told. And as for my invitation? Well that's really more Claire and Jen's doing than the bride-to-be, but here I am, joining the girls plus Becky's immensely beautiful, immensely tall sister, Holly, at Jen's house.

"This is more a summer residence," says Jen as she gives me a tour of the property. "It used to belong to my great aunt, and when she died, my parents gave it to me. I use it when I'm not working or at the weekends. My real home is in the city."

We stop in the master bedroom. There's a beautiful sea view. "I can see why you love it, though. It's a beautiful house."

"I miss the noise and the smells. I miss getting bagels for breakfast and the hustle and bustle of the New York sidewalk. This place has its charms, but it's not for me."

"I'd love to go one day, to the city. I've never been."

"Really?" She turns her head to one side as if she is trying to understand the strange creature before her. "Why?"

"When I was a kid, it was a lack of money, and as an adult, a lack of time, opportunity." I point at myself. "Real person, remember?"

She laughs. "Well, we'll have to fix that, won't we? You'll have to come visit." She gives me a shoulder hug, and we make our way back downstairs.

The large living room has been decorated with the most tasteless pink, helium-filled penis-shaped balloons available and a large sign that says, 'Same Penis Forever'. Well, if that isn't enough to put you off marriage forever, I don't know what will. The image of Hank's appendage flashes into my mind. I guess if I *have* to choose only one for the rest of my life, it wouldn't be the worst-case scenario.

"Who wants margaritas?" asks Claire, holding up a tray. She turns to look at my shocked face and winks at me. "I'm just serving the drinks tonight. You're kidding if I'm going to let a single drop of alcohol past these lips with Ted's baby inside me. I'd have the Secret Service battering down the door in seconds, orders of his family."

Holly giggles then thinks about it for a second. "They wouldn't really do that, would they?"

"Wouldn't be the first time. You should have seen what happened when Claire suggested they have coital relations out of wedlock," replies Becky, teasing her sister and receiving a pillow to the face for her troubles.

The doorbell rings. "Oh, that must be our guests."

Guests? I was led to believe that this is a quiet night in. I'd planned to get into some comfy pajamas and paint our toenails, wear masks and prepare for Becky's big day.

But somehow I've managed to forget that with these guys, everything is bigger, better and costs a ton of money. And to prove it, three extremely good-looking gentlemen, each wearing only a bow tie and an apron, strut in, swiftly followed by an army of people carrying food, drinks and a whole host of other items.

This is not the life I expected when I moved here, but I'm happy to partake.

"Ladies, these gentlemen are our butlers for the evening. They will be serving drinks and your every needs, well within limits." This isn't a comfy clothes and ponytail type of event, is it? I've totally misjudged the situation. Should have known better than to under-dress with these girls.

As if the good Lord hears my cry, Jen hands a pair of beautiful pink silk pajamas to each of us girls, personalized with our names on the front and 'Becky's Bachelorette' emblazoned on the back. "Go get changed, then the fun begins."

By the time we're all downstairs, half-naked men are serving canapés on silver trays, a group of women are setting up temporary pedicure stations and the margaritas are flowing.

Is this my life now? Despite the warm reception they've given me — well, most of them — our worlds are still miles apart. I've been invited because Hank and I are together, not because I actually belong. Like when you get a backstage pass for a concert and you spend the whole time moving out of the way for roadies and trying to see the artist from the side of the stage. All this privilege and yet you're not part of the game.

We sit in two rows, face to face, and get our feet beautified. I'm pretty sure the woman in charge of mine cringes a little when I pull off my socks. It's not like I've got gnarly nails or bunions or anything like that, but every inch of me hasn't been creamed and smoothed since birth, like the rest of the women. In fact, I spent the first twelve years of my life barefoot and homeschooled. She'll be earning her money tonight.

"This is the life," says Jen, as the butler hands her a perfectly cut sandwich and a glass of champagne. "I'd tip him, but I wouldn't know where to put it."

Becky places her hand on her butler's butt. "I can think of somewhere you can wedge it in."

"Becky!" says Claire, outraged. "You're not supposed to touch." She has a point. If the guys are doing the same thing with a group of scantily clad ladies at Ted's house right now, we'd be seriously offended.

The butler looks down at Becky, raises his eyebrows and bends over in front of her, shoving his butt in her face. "I don't mind."

Claire shakes her head as Becky slips a hundred dollar note in his butt crack and sends him on his way. Oh my God. I was not been expecting *this* when I was invited.

"So, Jen, how's it going with Chad?" asks Becky. All four friends have already sat and talked out their differences and indiscretions at a couple's retreat, as you do. Where I come from, Chad would have punched Jonny on the nose and they would never have spoken again, but here, after a cleansing ritual on the beach, a sexual rebirth and an open discussion about boundaries, they've all decided just to forget about it and move on.

Chad's TV show paying everybody handsomely to film the whole shebang probably didn't hurt. Rich people gotta rich.

"We've decided that we're not compatible as a couple," replies Jen, taking a huge bite out of her vegan, gluten-free pastry then wiping crumbs from her top.

"So you tried having an actual conversation with him then," says Becky, snark dripping from her mouth. "Because that's basically where it all went wrong for me."

"Yes," replies Jen. "The sex though..."

"Right? Jonny satisfies all of my needs, but my God that guy was a beast in bed."

Holly leans in. "So Chad's single now?"

"Ewww. Don't you even think about it." Becky squirms. "You're my sister. Eww, no, just no."

Jen giggles. "Yeah, that would seriously tip our group of friends into some sort of partner swapping cult and the Hamptons just aren't ready for that. Not publicly, anyway."

"And, Caitlyn, how are things with you and your boss...uh...I mean Hank?" asks Becky. Oh, she's on fine form tonight.

"Great," I reply. What am I supposed to say? That we can't keep our hands off of each other, that just the thought of him gets me hot and bothered.

"And the sex?"

I look over at Jen, cringing. "Uh...great?" The flush rises in my face.

"Because I think we can all agree that that guy's playing with some serious equipment."

"He'd need a longer apron, if he were to play butler for you, that's for sure," says Claire, joining in with the teasing for once.

I press my lips together. In my experience, the only way to deal with people like Becky, unless you know them as well as these women do, is to play along. I don't need to get her back up again, seeing as I've been given special permission to photograph her wedding tomorrow. "I certainly can't complain," I reply, raising my glass. "Cheers to great sex." Jen pretends to retch but holds up her glass anyway.

"That's the spirit. Although, be careful, you don't want to end up like Claire here, who hasn't seen her feet since March."

The mood is playful, and once we've finished with our feet, the butlers entertain us with a few party games. Their version of pin the tail on the donkey, with a life-size cardboard cutout of Jonny, is inspired.

A couple of hours later and we're all sitting around, perfectly sozzled. Claire is lain out on the couch and the rest of us are sitting on the floor. All the special guests have departed and only a few bottles of champagne remain, accompanied by an untouched selection of cakes that would blow your mind. I'm dying to dive in, but it's clear that neither an éclair nor a piece of sponge cake has passed these women's lips since childhood…and even then.

Someone knocks on the door. "More guests?" asks Becky.

Everyone shakes their heads. Jen stands up to go answer it, but from the rowdy voices, our late-night guests have already decided to come in.

The lads are here. Despite a strict 'boyfriend ban' imposed upon by Becky's parents, they've snuck over from Ted's house for a sneaky snuggle.

From the sound of crashing furniture, loud giggles then a collective 'Shhh', they are about as merry as we are.

Three heads pop around the door. Jen and Holly look at each other and roll their eyes. "I'm going to need another drink," says a sour-faced Jen.

"I'll join you." The two of them grab a bottle each and head upstairs. There's something so terribly comforting about not being the single girl right now. Not least that my drunken hunk of a boyfriend is looming toward me, arms open, lips puckered.

I've only ever experienced drunk Hank once before. Well, admittedly he was drunk and high, so it probably doesn't count, but it hadn't ended so well. Hopefully tonight will include less public nudity and more fornication in forbidden places.

"Hey, princess. You look so pretty." He fingers the collar of my silk pajamas, his hand sinking down to my chest. "You wanna go sit outside?" That Southern slur is back. *Hey, cowboy.*

"Okay." I grab a bottle of champagne and a whole frosted chocolate cake, stand and all. Well, I can't let it go to waste.

It's a warm night. It has to be late, around midnight, but the moon is out and the garden is lit with pretty lights leading down toward the beach. An old wooden building stands at the end of the garden. At home we'd have called it a shed, in comparison to the size of Jen's house, but it is in fact big enough for a British family of three.

Hank's tipsy retelling of the evening's adventures as he ambled down the garden, my hand in his, is utterly delightful. The men have had just as much fun as us.

"What is this place?" I ask as Hank fumbles around trying to find the hidden key.

"It's the boathouse, or at least it used to be. Jen wanted an office and reading room, so I did it up for her last year. It was one of my very first projects, just before I renovated the apartment." Key finally in hand, he unlocks the door and ushers me in.

"Oh my God it's beautiful." The inside is beautifully renovated, not at all the rickety spider filled cabin I'm expecting. The walls are lined with handmade bookshelves, just as he had done in his new property. To our left, Jen has installed a desk, looking out onto her garden and to our right, there's a large, comfy couch.

"Jen loves to read too. She's the one who got me into books when I was a kid." He walks over and opens the unfolding French doors, then pulls down a fitted mosquito net.

From the couch you can sit comfortably, a reading lamp overhead, book in hand, view of the ocean. Paradise.

Hank sits down on the couch and pulls me on top of him. "I have a confession to make."

"You do?" This doesn't bode well. Drunken Hank is often synonymous with horny Hank.

"Yes. Chad arranged for strippers at the party. I looked, and I tipped, but I didn't touch." He bows his head like a naughty schoolboy.

"We had nearly naked butlers. They might have gotten a few tips too." Head bent down, I peck him on the lips.

"What?" His jaw drops. "And you didn't..." He flashes a cheeky grin, but there's a hint of angst in his questioning. Jealous much?

"Touch? Maybe."

"Really?" His eyebrows shoot up.

"Of course not. And not just because I'm spoken for, but also because that's wrong. And you didn't get a lap dance, I suppose? I find that hard to believe."

He scrunches up his nose. "No. The other guys really wanted me to, but it's never really been my thing."

"And?"

"And all I could think about was you, obviously." Two could play at the teasing game.

"Obviously." I thrust my pelvis forward, sashay my hips, swaying from side to side over his crotch. "I could give you one now if you like."

Arms raised above my head, I writhe around, grinding onto him until his cock is bursting to get out of his pants. I shimmy my breasts into his face, rolling back my shoulders and pushing the tips of my nipples against his mouth. He's really getting into it, clumsily kissing my chest and opening my pajamas button by button.

"I thought you didn't like lap dances."

He looks up at me, gasping as I grind down into him. "I could get a taste for them."

Grabbing his curly locks, I pull his head back and kiss him hard, devouring him.

The control arouses me. I'm in charge, for once, and that excites me to my core. The more he groans and writhes beneath me, *wanting* me, the wetter I get.

I lean back, grabbing his shoulders and inspecting the fine specimen of a man before me, taking a moment to enjoy the view. He lifts his hand and ruffles his hair back into place. "You got a new watch?" It's flashy, like perfume advert flashy.

"Oh this. It was a gift for the groomsmen." That little gift must have cost the price of a family car.

Becky had given a gift to her wedding party tonight too—jewelry, makeup, expensive lingerie. Basically, everything they all had free and easy access to at home. They'd opened them in front of me.

It stings being left out in that way, constantly reminded of my place. Tomorrow I will go back to being an employee and while they party the day away, I'll have to content myself with watching it all from thirty feet away.

I grab Hank's shirt and rip it open, leaning back and savoring his perfect pecs, the glisten of sweat on his creased abs. I unbutton his pants and release his cock, grabbing the shaft and slowly swirling my thumb around the tip. I might not be in charge of many things in my life right now, but I am the captain of the boathouse.

Stepping off, I drop my silk pants to the floor revealing a sexy little lacy thong. I'd like to say I've dressed for the occasion, but it was the last thing in my underwear drawer. I'd brought it with me to the US on a whim and I still hadn't caught up on my laundry. It chafes and pulls at all the wrong places, but from the look on Hank's face, it's having the desired effect. I whisk it off and throw it in the air, standing naked before him.

He pulls a condom out of his back pocket and I grab it, ripping it open with my teeth. This gets that little drunken chuckle out of him that I'd fallen for on the plane and my heart melts. If only he knew just how much I loved him.

But that was never the goal, and it can never happen. I bite my lip and my frustration turns up a notch.

I have that condom on him in seconds, climbing back over him and sliding down onto his impressive cock. We've not yet done it with me on top, but any worries I have about being too shallow for him disappear as he fills me to my core.

My arousal peaks and I pleasure myself with my fingers as I slowly ride up and down on him, making myself come with such ease. As I tighten around him, my body shivering in pleasure, he moans so loudly that I have to kiss it right out of him. No need to wake the neighbors.

I increase my rhythm, placing his hands on my butt to help me as my legs grow tired. Faster and faster I fuck him, easing the nervous tension out of my body, turning my anger into something wild and liberated.

My hands firmly gripping his shoulders, his moans intensify. I pump up and down, faster and faster, until his whole body stiffens beneath me.

But still, I carry on, as he releases, riding and riding him, harder and harder.

"Caitlyn, stop." He puts his hands on my hips and holds me to him. "You're hurting me."

I look down at his confused, wounded face and slide back to release him from my grasp.

"Sorry." Fuck. "Oh my God. Shit, sorry." I put my hand to my mouth, ashamed by my selfishness. Sex is a two-player game.

The tears are a release. I sit there, balanced on his lap, and sob my heart out. He pulls me in to him with his strong, comforting arms, holding my crying, naked body against his.

He wipes a tear from my cheek and peers into my eyes. "What's going on, Caitlyn?"

"I'm sorry. I just don't feel like I'm in control of anything at the moment. This whole…situation, the lying, Becky and her biting remarks about us, it's all too much. I'm so sorry. I didn't want to hurt you. I got carried away." Lying to his family, lying to him. I'm constantly having to check myself.

"It's fine. It's just, you know, that you've got to stop when it's over. You didn't *hurt* hurt me. It just chafed a bit." He pushes me up, removes the condom, ties it up and chucks it onto the floor, then checks himself before pulling me back to his chest. "I'm sorry you've got the rough end of the stick, if you'll excuse the pun. But I've got some good news that might cheer you up. I think I've sold my house."

"You did?" I can't help but grin at him through my snotty, tear-stained face. This is what he's been working so hard for, and my heart bursts with pride. "Did you get what you wanted for it?"

"They didn't even haggle. It means I can give up the magazine, on the agreement that you keep your job, of course, and start out on my own, with my own money. I've known for a week or so, but I didn't want to tell you until I was sure. I sign on Monday."

I'll keep my job? Not a hope in hell. As soon as he announces to the world that he is going into the hammer-and-nails business full-time, I will be out on my ear. I take a deep breath. Hank lives in his fantasy world where everything will turn out all right. It almost feels like this is a game sometimes, this war between him and his parents. And I'm a pawn.

I throw my smile back on my face. I've already taken out enough frustration on this guy for one night. "That is so exciting. And here's me being a Debbie Downer, when we should be celebrating." I stepped off of him and slipped my clothes back on. "How about we open that bottle of champagne and do dirty things with chocolate frosting? Then we can sit here and watch the sun come up and you can tell me all about your next project."

He pulls me back down onto his lap and kisses me, so sweetly it makes me want to cry again. "I can't imagine my life without you," he says as he tucks my hair behind my ear. "Any woman who will happily let me talk drywall and drains, she's a keeper."

Chapter Twenty

Caitlyn

Wedding Day. I'm up early to capture photos of the flurry of hairstylists, makeup artists and the battalion of beauty providers. The bride and her party are already preened and primped on a normal day. How could they possibly improve on that? From the looks of things, it is going to involve temporary hair extensions and under-eye masks to try to make them all look a little less like they haven't slept a wink all night.

Becky rushes from room to room screaming, "I'm getting married today!" while everyone queues for the shower.

"You have a leaf in your hair," I say, plucking half a tree out of the nest of hair on Claire's head.

"You have boathouse on your ass," replies Claire, raising her eyebrows.

"Sorry, what?" How does she know?

"They don't soundproof boathouses. I think everybody on the street knows what you did last night."

"The boathouse, huh?" says Jen, joining the queue. "Ah, young love! I hope you tidied up after yourselves. What about you, Claire? What devastation did you do in my beautiful garden?"

"That old swing-set will never be the same."

"Eww, guys, TMI!" says Becky, coming to see why there's a traffic jam in the hallway. "Who's in there? They're taking ages."

"Well, unless it's Holly, I think we have an intruder."

"Someone call my name?" asks Holly, as she walked out of the bathroom in only a skimpy thong.

"Ugh, that woman is a masterpiece," says Claire, watching Holly slink back to her room. "I used to look like that."

"Claire, you are beautiful, you are giving life to a child, now concentrate please. Five-minute shower, hair washed only if you've been instructed to have wet hair by the hairstylist. Go, girls, go. Time is ticking!"

By ten they are all in their matching wedding bathrobes, undies on, hair in rollers, getting their nails and makeup done.

Claire and Holly are checking out the photos the boys have been posting on social media all morning, looking so gorgeous in their dark blue tuxes and bowties.

The dresses had been delivered first thing. The bouquets have arrived too, bunches of white flowers, each tied up with a simple blue ribbon.

The cars are due at eleven, and by ten-forty-five, they are all standing in the living room, waiting for the blushing bride.

Becky floats down the stairs, looking perfect — not a hair out of place, not a pimple or a smudge.

It hadn't been easy, convincing everybody to accept that she wasn't marrying Chad, but she is too excited about finally marrying the love of her life to let anything bring her down. I smile at her, bending down to take a full-length photo. "You look beautiful. Jonny's going to be so proud."

She heads toward her girls, arms wide open, for a group hug. But the wedding organizer, furious, runs over, ripping her from their arms. "No hugging!" The risk of makeup smudging has been elevated to a code red.

As we enter Becky's parents' house, most of the guests have already arrived and are seated. The groom is nervously waiting with his best men, checking that they have all remembered what to do and who has the rings.

I swirl around discretely, taking natural photos of everybody. I'm going to have some great shots.

The wedding organizer arrives and informs Jonny that it is time to go and await his bride by the altar. "Chad, you will now be walking the bride's sister down the aisle, so the order is, you and Holly, then Hank with Jen, then Ted with Claire. Everyone got that? Good. Remember, slow steps in rhythm. Don't fuck it up. Those are the bride's words, not mine."

Jonny hurries off. They all stand in the salon, which leads out to the garden where the entire riches of the Hamptons are seated, starting to roast in the midday heat. I spot Hank and take a second to admire my man.

He is adjusting his tie, trying to stop his wavy Italian curls from flopping in front of his face. I've never seen him in a tuxedo before, and I'm not disappointed. The way his trousers curve sublimely around his tight little butt and the jacket, how it flatters his broad shoulders, his biceps bursting to get out. Is it so bad that all I can imagine is ripping it off of him?

He looks up, grins at me, sensing I am devouring him with my eyes, then he checks me out and nods.

Are we both doing-it in our heads right now? Very possibly.

The organizer grabs Chad and Holly and links her arm through his. "You start walking slowly when the music starts. When these two arrive at the altar, the next couple leaves. Got it? Good! As the bride would say…"

"Don't fuck it up!" they chorus and the organizer blushes.

"Quietly," he adds, out of the side of his mouth.

I rush down to the middle of the aisle, crouching down to avoid bothering anybody.

The music begins, and Chad and Holly start walking toward me. "So I hear you and Jen didn't work out," says Holly. "So you're, like single?" She flutters her eyelids and gives him her most seductive smile.

Snake.

Jen loops her arm into Hank's. Off they go. "Seriously, the boathouse? Do you have no shame?"

"The swing set was already occupied," replies Hank, winking at me as they drift past.

They go left and right at the altar and Claire and Ted start waddling down. "Did you remember to feed Mr. Whiskers this morning?" asks Claire.

"Yeah, you know he pooped right next to the litter tray again," he replies, causing his wife to roll her eyes.

The wedding is romantic but long, as weddings are. The afternoon reception is, of course, a grand affair. The guests are seated in a huge marquee, with enough place settings for four hundred people. There are six courses, a speech between every course.

Ted and Hank deliver the best men's speeches, being the only people not involved in the very convoluted love story that has brought Jonny and Becky together. In fact, the very nature of their relationship makes it very difficult for the two men to reference it, so they just tell some funny old stories about Jonny's teenage and college years and leave it at that.

As the wedding party disperses for a couple of hours to relax in their rooms before the evening reception, I pack up my things and prepare to leave. I catch up with Hank as he heads upstairs. "I'll see you tomorrow. Have fun tonight, and behave yourself."

"Wait, stay. I have a room." He checks that we're alone. "You don't have to go yet, right?" Snaking his hand around my waist, he pulls me into a nook and pecks me on the lips. "Pretty please."

"You are incorrigible. But I could do with a nap after last night's shenanigans."

I follow him up to his room.

"I have a surprise for you." He's all excited.

"In your room? Did you put a bow tie on your dick?"

"No. Damn it, remind me to get them for our wedding." Our wedding? He says these things sometimes. The man is a conundrum. Pulling me into his room, he then locks the door behind us. "This is for you."

"It's a dress. Why do I need a dress?"

"Becky asked me to ask you to the party tonight." He lifts his hands. "I swear this is nothing to do with what happened last night. She and the girls organized the whole thing. They knew inviting you to the ceremony would be tricky, but they wanted to make sure you knew how much a part of our group you are."

I gulp back my joy. "Really?" The dress is beautiful. Green silk, lined. It has to have cost a pretty fortune. "I don't know what to say, except that you guys have gone and bought me more clothes. You really need to stop. I—" I stop myself. Say the thing. Tell him.

"Say yes. Be my plus one tonight. Dance with me. It doesn't feel right when you're not there." Oh, he is on form tonight if he wants to make me cry.

He takes my hand and leads me into the shower. "Wait."

"I know. You can't get your hair wet. I do pay attention." He grabs the showerhead, waits until the water is perfect and rinses my body in warm water. Then he grabs the shower gel and soaps me from head to toe, paying special attention to areas which, in his opinion, need more scrubbing than others.

Why he thinks my breasts are so dirty, I have no idea.

Once I've been rinsed off, he towel dries me and pulls me onto the bed.

"What is all of this?"

"You have been an angel. You have put up with my family, my friends and their bizarre lifestyles and love triangles. My total incapacity to know how to be in a relationship without making you cry. Tonight it's all about you."

He spreads my legs and places a warm, hard tongue on my clit. My breath hitches. Nobody has ever done this before, made it all about me.

* * * *

As we step out of our room a couple of hours later, there's a commotion in the corridor. Ted, Claire, Jen, Becky and Jonny as well as several other guests, are gathered in front of one of the bedrooms.

"Yes, yes, yes!" screams a female voice, followed by a crash, a bang and several moans of pleasure in a much deeper tone.

"Whose room is this?" asks Hank, raising his eyebrows in admiration. We'd just been doing something similar a few doors down. Had anybody heard us too?

"It's Holly's room. It's been going on for twenty minutes, unbelievable. Half my family have walked past here for one reason or another. She's hardly discreet." Becky is fuming. This is not the day to steal her thunder. Holly and whoever is in there with her are in serious trouble. As the passion inside the room comes to a crescendo, Holly's cries became louder and louder and frankly a lot more vulgar until a male voice cries out, "Bail out!" Becky and Jen look at each other.

"Holy shit!" says Jen, cringing, "He's doing *that*, on her."

Becky screeches, "Fucking hell, Chad! Holly, stop that immediately!" The sound of scrambling and cursing can be heard from inside. A straggly, out of breath Holly opens the door.

"Fuck off, Becky. I'm busy." She sees the crowd and tries to close the door, but Becky steps forward, wedging her foot in.

"Don't you close that door on me. Tell Chad to get dressed, then he can get out of my house and out of our lives. What were you thinking?"

Holly opens the door wider, a set of straps barely covering her assets. "I was bored, and you were getting all the attention. I wasn't planning on keeping him."

"Well, thanks a fucking lot," says Chad, opening the door fully in only trousers and socks, dressing himself as he storms off.

"Don't let the door hit you on the way out," shouts Becky.

We all stand there in the hallway, nervously awaiting instructions from our hosts.

"What are the straps for?" asks Claire.

"Not here, Claire. Not today." Becky grabs her husband's arm, whispers sweet nothings in his ear, acting more like his sweet wife than the bridezilla she'd been a few minutes ago.

"But is it any good?" she asks Jen.

"I couldn't possibly say," she replies, glancing nervously at her brother. Hank and Ted walk away and Claire and I hold back, desperate to know. "Fucking incredible, and that parachute? Ingenious."

I am starting to see why Chad is so very popular among the ladies of this group.

Chapter Twenty-One

Caitlyn

By the time we get downstairs Becky has calmed down and is happily chatting away to friends and family. The happy couple are invited onto the dance floor to open the ball, then the ushers and bridesmaids join them. Holly doesn't make an appearance. She'll be persona non grata tonight, anyway, knowing Becky.

It's lovely, just waltzing around on a warm summer's night. Hank's dance lessons with his grandma paid off. With one arm tightly wound around my waist the other holding my hand in the air, he whisks me around that dance floor like the slightly less dirty bits in *Dirty Dancing*.

"You know, you look so beautiful in that dress. It's going to be almost a shame to rip it off you later."

"Me? Look at you. Damn, Enrico Baresi, that bowtie is doing things to me you couldn't even imagine." I play with his curls. It's my favorite move, just before I pull his head down to mine and kiss him.

Except of course we can't. Because I am a secret. I shouldn't even be here, on the dance floor. Becky might have made an exception, inviting me to spend the evening, but for all intents and purposes, I am just a friend. And Hank's employee.

The Baresi parents' eyes bore into the back of my head. Nonna is surely scowling and remembering past loves. If she had to suffer then so do we all, apparently, even if we aren't in 1950 anymore.

Hank slides his arm tighter around my waist, pulling me to him. His semi-hard cock pushes against my body. I gasp for breath, pushing away the desire to rub against him, but he spins me around and does it himself.

"You're such a tease, Baresi," I say. "You're going to get us in trouble."

"Do you like it when I'm bad. Do I need to be punished?" he whispers in my ear, before letting out a frustrated moan. "You weren't complaining earlier on."

I sure hadn't been. If he hadn't made it all about me earlier, he might not be such a horny devil right now. He's thirsty as hell. "Stop it."

"But I love you," he says, whirling me around once again.

"What?" I throw my head back, stare into his eyes. *Did I just hear him right?*

He puts his forehead on mine. "I said I love you because I do. You get me. You get my friends, even when they're thoroughly misbehaving. Even my sister refers to you as *the sister I never had,* and she's already got several sisters-in-law."

"I…" I don't quite know what to say.

"I don't have a lot of experience in this kind of thing, but aren't you supposed to reciprocate or something, or have I got this whole thing wrong?"

"No." I laugh and stretch up toward him, on my highest tippy-toes. "I love you, Enrico Baresi. I've loved you since you lay down next to me and showed me the stars."

"You have?" The delight in his face is reward enough for allowing myself to open up to him a little. I've not been entirely truthful, and we are going to have to talk about things, eventually, but here, now, tonight the man who holds my heart has proclaimed his love for me. This is not the time or place for bringing down the mood.

"Of course. You just needed more time to work it out in your head."

Our lips meet. Everyone around us evaporates, just Hank and I melding together. I melt into him as if the warmth of his body thaws my ice-cold heart.

How ridiculous it seems now, as I dance with the man who loves me, that I had sworn to never fall in love again. Laughable. No bad boys, no relationships that wouldn't ever work and yet on the very day I'd caught the plane I'd met someone who would become both everything I want and simultaneously, in so many ways, epitomize everything I hoped to avoid. Yet love prevailed.

The most precious of moments, our first 'I love you' should be magical and yet as we dance and kiss on the most romantic of occasions, a thundering smash brings us out of our reverie.

Everybody turns to look.

Guillermo Baresi crashes his fist on the table a second time, sending several glasses hurtling to their deaths. Mama tries as best she can to mop it up with serviettes, but he lifts a hand and she backs away. The waiters will do it. Those who serve. *People like me.*

The scowl on his face is monumental. That of an angry, bitter man.

His children do not kiss their employees in front of hundreds of his friends and neighbors. His children do not bring shame upon the family name. But here he is, throwing a childish tantrum in front of the world, and that's okay because he's the boss.

The fact that everybody else's grown children are sleeping with each other, sniffing coke in the bathroom and selling their lives on reality TV is neither here nor there.

There are rules, and we have broken them. Somebody will have to pay.

Hank looks over at his father, then back at me. What are we going with right now? Defiance? Regret? I'm ready to follow whatever lead Hank wants to take. He takes my face in his hands, looks deep into my soul and plants the most sensual, overtly passionate kiss on my lips.

Defiance it is, then.

"Basta!" Out of the corner of my eye, I spot Guillermo Baresi barreling toward us, arms flailing. I pull away from Hank. He looks up, swipes his arm around me, pushing me behind him, instinctively protecting me.

"Papa, you're embarrassing yourself," he says, looking down at his angry, red-faced father. I grab Hank's hand and he holds me so tightly, his thumb rubbing my palm, reassuring me. My heart is beating out of my chest, and everybody is staring at us. I hate it. I hate being so visible and I'm starting to regret ever coming. I could have changed the outcome of this, with one little conversation. I could have made this all better, but I didn't. What have I done?

Guillermo replies in Italian and Hank ripostes with a gesture that I know to be offensive. It gets heated, both of them shouting at each other in Italian, arms waving, voices raised. "We should just leave," I say, but nobody hears me.

Becky, however, is never ignored. Neither are her parents. Forces of nature to equal any warring Italian families, they make short sharp shrift of the incident, calling security to accompany both Hank and his father out of the ballroom. His hand is ripped from mine as two hefty men in black suits suggest, rather forcefully, that they take this outside.

Hank's mother is waiting outside in the car. She doesn't utter a word to us, insisting to her husband that they leave immediately. Dust flies into the air as they speed away and we stand on the gravel driveway, rather lost after such a heated moment. Both bursting with adrenaline and no way to bring us down.

"I have something I need to tell you," I say to Hank.

"Not right now. I need to think." He turns to me. "You were right, cutting off meant cutting off my family too." Wealth, families, it just brings people pain. I hate it. I hate it so much.

"Please, I really want to talk about this." He doesn't listen he grabs my hand and heads for the car.

"I'll drive," I say. "You've had a couple of drinks. I'll come back and get our stuff tomorrow." I reach into my purse and grab my keys. Everything will be better tomorrow. Our minds will be clearer and we'll be able to talk.

* * * *

They say your memory deliberately takes away the details of an accident. You don't remember because the trauma is so extreme. But as I lie there, every second of that truck hitting my car is etched into my mind. The crunch of metal on metal, the sensation of flying. The thought that flashes through your mind as your car careens into another and another, *'people don't get out of this type of accident alive'*.

There is shouting. But it isn't me. The glass in my driver's side window is gone. I can see people rushing around. Other cars have stopped. It doesn't hurt. I just can't seem to move. People are talking, calling emergency services.

"She came out of nowhere," says a man. Is he the truck driver?

Me? Was it me? Had I come out of nowhere? I'd gotten confused, trying to find the house. I'd been there a few times, admittedly, but I still wasn't used to America, to driving on the wrong side of the road, on the wrong side of the car. Is it my fault?

"Are you okay?" A woman is talking to me. I look at the woman. Am I awake? A burning smell irritates my nose.

There are sirens. Someone is still shouting. *Be quiet.* Am I in trouble, has somebody called the police? I might have been driving on the wrong side of the road.

"Ma'am you've been in an accident. Can you tell me your name?"

Is he going to arrest me? I don't want to go to prison.

"Caitlyn Walsh, her name is Caitlyn Walsh." Hank. I look down. He's holding my hand. It's all bloody. He's hurt. I look at his face. No, he's fine.

People are shouting behind the police officer. Are they angry? Am I in trouble?

Hank is here. He will tell them not to arrest me. I close my eyes. I can rest now that Hank is here to save the day.

Chapter Twenty-Two

Hank

Bashed-up cars litter the street. An impromptu junkyard. The sound of steel cutting through steel makes my teeth hurt. They are trying to get Caitlyn out. My face hurts from the airbag, but I don't even care.

A cop pulled me from the car, sat me here. "The firefighters are going to cut her out. Don't move." He leaves me there on the street. I don't want to, I won't leave here until I know she's okay. This is my fault. All of it. Making her drive, forcing her to stay at the party tonight when she wanted to go home earlier. My family, my problem. She should never have to have been involved. I wanted to show the world that I was in love, show off my beautiful girlfriend, but instead I led her into the crocodile's mouth.

"Caitlyn." I try to stand, but it's like wading through water. My whole body is shaking. My legs give way once again.

"Sir, you need to sit down. You can't help her. Do you have someone you can call?" I look down at my phone. Who? My family? No way. This is *his* doing.

I call Ted. "Tell them to take her to Gacilly," he says. "They have the best ER." I tell him to stay at the party, and that I'll keep in touch.

They slowly lift her out onto a stretcher, and the cop allows me over. I just want to pick her up and take her away from all of this, make it better. That's my job.

"Are you her next of kin?" asks the paramedic.

"Yes." And she is mine.

I walk alongside them as they speed toward the ambulance. "She was very lucky. The car took the brunt of the hit. There are no visible broken bones. Several cuts and bruises. My colleagues at the hospital will check for internal injuries, and we'll need to do an MRI."

We get in the ambulance and they wheel her in. Mask over her mouth, connected up to machines, an IV in her hand, she doesn't look lucky. My heart is as broken as the woman before me. How could this have happened?

Her hand clenches mine. "Caitlyn." She opens her eyes, tries to get up. "No, no, you need to lie down. We're going to the hospital, honey. They're going to make you better." Her heartbeat increases, her eyes widen in fear.

The paramedic pushes me aside. "Caitlyn, you need to breathe." He takes deep breaths. "That's it, deep breaths." The beeping slows. He moves away then lets me back in. "Positive affirmations. Deep breaths, huh?"

I nod. "I love you so much." I close my eyes. Baresis don't cry. Might as well be a family mantra. We get up, and we get on with it. Hammered into my brain since forever. I choke the tears down. I can cry later. Positive affirmations. "I'm right here, and I'm not going anywhere."

Chapter Twenty-Three

Caitlyn

"Cait." Hank's voice is muffled. "Jen, call the nurse. She's waking up. Cait, can you hear me?"

I open my eyes. Hank is looming over me, my hand in his. A sense of calm fills me, whether it's him or a certain quantity of morphine I'm not sure. Nevertheless, I'm good.

We're in the hospital. That particular mix of pine and chemicals.

"You okay?" It comes out rough, like I've swallowed sandpaper. I rub my throat and he hands me a glass of water, helping me lean forward to drink it.

"No. But don't worry about that or anything else. Let's just worry about you."

He has reason to worry. My body feels like one huge bruise. I lift my hand to my head. "Don't touch it," says Jen from behind him. "Stitches."

I nod and put my hand down. "Thanks."

A woman in scrubs comes in and pushes everyone out of the way. "What's going on here then? You're a popular young lady. Let's have a look at you." She shines a light into my eyes. "What day is it today?"

I have to think about it. What did I do this morning? Yesterday. "Saturday, probably Sunday by now."

"Good. Now follow the light." My head spins as she makes my eyes jerk from left to right and back again. She holds up a pen. "Grab the pen, please." Is there tequila in my drip? It takes three tries, but I get it in the end.

"Everything seems as we suspected. A very mild concussion. No bones broken, but you are going to hurt all over for a few days at least." She turns to Hank. "I'm going to keep her in overnight. You can pick her up tomorrow, but no driving and calm for a few days at least."

"Thank you so much," says Hank, grabbing my hand back in his.

"I've got to get back too, plus I've got a million messages from everyone wanting to know if you're all right. I'll come see you soon, okay."

Hank puts out his free hand to grab hers and turns away for a second. "Thank you, Jen." Tears fill his eyes. "You don't know what it means, you being here. Take…" He pauses. "Take care of yourself." Hank Baresi, king of the unsaid words. I might have bashed my brain, but I know how much he loves his sister and I know if his father has his way, we won't be seeing her again.

I lie back into my pillow and close my eyes. My head is pounding and the room spins, but I have enough coherent thought to remember what happened today.

His face is red from crying. This is all my fault. We could have died.

"I'm sorry." It doesn't even begin to encompass the regret I'm feeling right now.

"No, no, no. You have nothing to be sorry about. I shouldn't have made you drive home. I was so angry." He climbs up onto the bed, next to me. Delicately reaching behind me, he pulls me into a gentle hug. "You scared the shit out of me. How you survived that crash, I will never know. You can't do that to me ever again, do you understand? My poor heart can't take it."

I laugh. "Ouch." It hurts to even breathe, let alone use any other muscles. "Trust me, I have absolutely no intention of ever having my car hit head-on by a truck again. You have my solemn word." That split second when I thought we were going to die will come back to haunt me for the rest of my life.

He kisses the top of my head. "Caitlyn, I love you."

I snuggle into him. "I know. I have to tell you something. I'm so tired." I can hardly keep my eyes open and the warm embrace of Hank's arms is sending me back to sleep.

"It can wait. Get some sleep. I'm going to go get changed. I will be back later. Don't go anywhere."

I close my eyes and nestle into him. "You're funny. Don't go until I'm asleep. You're warm and you smell like love."

* * * *

I'm woken by movement. It's still dark outside, and somebody has put on a bedside light. "Hank?"

"I don't think anybody has ever compared me to my youngest son. He takes after his mother's side of the family."

I open my eyes, wide. Guillermo Baresi. Who the fuck let him in? What am I thinking, he probably owns the place.

"What do you want?" I turn away from him. He's an evil little man, and he scares me. I'm about as vulnerable as I can be right now and he knows it.

"I think we need to have a chat." Only a chat? Well, that's a relief, I'd half expected him to grab a pillow and stuff it over my face. Finish the job.

"I have nothing to say to you."

"I'm going to make you a proposition, one you can't refuse." *Oh, please.* My head hurts too much for this rich guy's shit.

"Oh, I think I can refuse. Leave me alone. Never come back. See, easy-peasy?"

He leans over me, squeezes my shoulder so tight it has to leave a mark. "I told you I would destroy you. I told you that if you did not leave my son alone, if you continued to encourage him in his stupid little pursuits, you would regret it."

I grab the call button, press it. "So you sent your favorite truck driver to deal with me."

He moves back, releases his grip. "Oh, you silly little girl. I don't hurt people physically. I don't have to. And I would never harm my son." I press the call button again. "The nurse isn't coming. She's busy."

Okay, now he's starting to scare me.

I grab my water. Staying calm and in control is the key here. "Say what you have to say, then leave."

"I will give you two options. You can stay, keep pretending that you're in love with my son, even though he's no longer worth anything to you. But let me be very clear, you will never work in media again. Ever. Anywhere. And Hank? He will never see his family again. I will make sure that his beloved mother does not utter another word to him until she goes to her grave, which, let's be honest, without her darling Enrico, is going to be an early one."

I think of my mother, of that cold church. The first place Hank had ever taken me to was lunch with his mother. He's always joking about how he's the favorite. Guillermo is absolutely right. It would kill her.

"His mother would never do that."

"Oh my poor girl, you underestimate me. My wife will do exactly as I say. You see, she quite likes her life exactly as it is. She knows what would happen if she defied me."

That poor, sweet woman. After everything Hank has told me about his parents' relationship, my heart breaks for her.

I sit back and take a breath. "You're so occupied with money that you don't even see people, do you? If you did, you would realize that whether Hank has a penny to his name makes no difference to me."

He snorts. "Shut up. As if I haven't dealt with your kind before. I haven't even begun. I have friends in high places. That house of his will be declared unfit for sale. It won't be worth a penny. You won't only be broke, you'll be in debt. Enrico will soon be left behind by everybody he loves. His precious friends won't find him so interesting once he's got no money in the bank. This lifestyle doesn't come cheap. A little word in the ear of my golf buddies and their sons will no longer be so keen on keeping in touch. He brought shame on his family and they would not wish to do the same"

He can't do that, can he? He has a point though. Chad, Jonny, Ted, they all depend on their parents. That would be so incredibly cruel. But cruelty is the point, isn't it?

'I will destroy you,' he'd said.

My head hurts. I lie back down, close my eyes. "What's the second option?" No, really, I'm *dying* to know.

"Ah, you see, I knew you couldn't refuse. You sign this little piece of paper I have in my hand. Ten million of the finest American dollars in your bank account by midnight tonight."

My heart races. I can't believe I'm even asking this. "And what would I get for my money?"

"In one week you leave here and never come back. You never talk to my son again and you don't tell him about our agreement. He gets to keep his friends, his family, even that stupid little property he loves so much."

My head is pounding. I just want him to leave. "Really? He gets to do the job he loves?" I doubt that.

"Of course not, a Baresi in construction? Don't be ridiculous, girl."

I look at him. This sweaty, little pig of a man, willing to ruin his son for loving the wrong woman. How many times has he done this to another of his sons? Just how deep will his relentless need to control his children go? He is reveling in this, smiling as he buys off the greedy little gold-digger. Ten million dollars is nothing to this man. Small Change.

"No, thank you." I smile at him. "I'm sure we'll be just fine."

"What?"

"We'll take our chances." His face contorts into rage.

"You stupid, fucking little bitch. Just take the fucking money." He's so shocked and angry, like a child having a tantrum.

I begin to laugh. First a chuckle, then louder and harder until I'm cackling away, holding my sides from the pain. He's so angry that he can't bear it, and he lifts his fist.

"I wouldn't do that if I were you." Hank steps into the room, and he tightens his hand around his father's wrist. "Get out."

"You deserve each other." His father spits it out. He grabs back his hand.

"Out!" screams Hank. He's white as a sheet, his hands balled into fists.

His father smirks. "You'll come running back when you need the money." He walks out.

Hank rushes to my side. "Are you okay? Did he hurt you?"

This poor guy is having a day of it.

"I'm fine. He doesn't scare me." It's a lie, but I'm more concerned about Hank than ever before and I just want to sleep off this headache. "I want to go home and look at the stars with you. I don't want to stay here anymore." His father has me rattled. He's not used to people saying no. I've gone too far. I need us both to feel safe tonight and the only safe place around here is in Hank's arms.

"Whatever you want. I'm going to get the nurse. I'll be back straight away, I promise."

I nod. If there's one thing I'm sure of, Guillermo Baresi will never hurt his son again. I will make sure of that.

Unfortunately, I can't say the same for myself.

Chapter Twenty-Four

Hank

She's home. As much as this house can be considered a home. The downstairs bedroom here is more practical than the apartment. I canceled the sale. It can wait. The most important thing is making sure Caitlyn is okay, safe.

"Good morning." We had fallen asleep hand in hand last night, her body too pained for hugging. I push her hair off of her face. Even covered in cuts and bruises, she is beautiful.

She smiles, and everything is right in the world. "Do you know what happened yesterday?" she asks. "You told someone you loved them for the very first time." Her smile grows, and she tips her head to the side, maybe waiting for an encore.

"I did," I reply. "And then I said it to you." She goes to thwack me on the arm, but can't even lift hers.

"Everything hurts. This sucks. Plus, I need a shower."

"There's a bath in the en suite or showers upstairs." Her eyes light up. "You want a bath, don't you? Right. Give me five minutes."

The warm water runs into the foam, forming huge soapy clouds. The smell of roses fills the room. I undo her robe, let it fall to the ground. She stands naked in front of me.

"I have never had so many bruises in my life." She's all colors of the rainbow, with cuts down her arms from the shattered glass. I hide my discomfort. We'll play pretend for now, like everything is okay. I don't want her worrying about my problems. Her health comes first. Everything else can wait.

I wish I hadn't been so giving yesterday. I'm horny as fuck for her. I imagine sliding my hands down her back, running my fingers along the little curve of her spine and grabbing that butt. Those boobs, I just want to bury my head into them, dive right in. My hand sinks to my dick and I readjust myself. She's getting me hard just looking at her.

"You're still hot as hell."

She giggles coyly. "Nurse Hank, you're supposed to be in charge of making me better. You heard the doctor. No sex."

"I still can't believe you asked the doctor. No, I take that back. Nothing that comes out of your mouth ever surprises me."

"I love you, cowboy."

I cackle. That stupid nickname... She's never going to let me forget it. Okay, she's got me, the whole love thing. That's going to take some getting used to. We've said it now. I can believe it.

"I love you, too, princess."

Pulling my T-shirt over my head, and unbuttoning my jeans, I strip down to my boxers. She gulps, her eyes moving up and down my body. "You're getting in with me?"

"It's not a Jacuzzi. I just don't want to get my clothes wet."

"Yeah, it would be a shame if you got all soapy," she replies, winking at me.

"No sex, Caitlyn. Orders of Nurse Hank, and I must be obeyed." She rolls her eyes, sulking. We're like dogs in heat.

"Well, crap, it seems like such a waste, me being bedridden and all." She stumbles slightly, putting her hand out to steady herself.

"Let's get you washed." I sink my hands delicately behind her thighs and lift her, letting her sink into the hot, soapy water. A face towel in my hand, I kneel down, wet it in the soapy water and slowly drip it onto her hair, avoiding the stitches on her scalp. Then squeeze a little shampoo onto my hand and massage her head.

"Oh God, this is amazing, better than sex." She giggles and pushes her head against my hands.

"Oh yeah? Looks like I need to work on my technique."

She turns her head, kisses my soapy forearm. "Nah, you're good."

I squirt shower gel onto my hand, sit her up and run my fingers up and down her back, to groans of delight. I'm not averse to a back rub myself. There will definitely be payback at some point. It's only fair. This is the second time I've bathed this woman in two days.

I lie her back down and rub soap from her shoulder to her arm, each motion as delicate as I can. She flinches at every touch. Her hands are so dainty, her nails, so pretty for the wedding, are now scratched and broken. When we have money again, when the house is sold, I'm going to treat her to the best manicure in town, no expense spared. She deserves the world and one day I'm going to give it to her.

Her feet are so pretty. That pedicure at Becky's house the other day did wonders. I've never known someone who hates footwear as much as Caitlyn. The minute she is inside, her shoes and socks come off. My barefoot princess. She sinks back down into the bath, her eyes closed, and lets out a pleasured moan.

"Oh my God, that is incredible."

Something on her foot catches my eye. "You have a tattoo?"

"It's Latin. *Perserva*. It means 'keep going'. It reminds me that no matter how hard it gets, how difficult life is, you've just got to stand up and keep walking. Don't give up." She lifts her head, looks at me. "I want you to always remember that. Sometimes bad things happen for good reasons. Never give up."

"A touch too philosophical for me." I laugh. I still haven't heard from my family. As long as I have Caitlyn, I'll make it through. I made my choices.

I slowly trace my fingers up her leg. She's fit, not like a runner, but well defined. Her thighs are covered in fine little hairs. I long for the moment I can trace my tongue up her thigh and taste her sweet pussy. This is going to be the longest week of my life. Why didn't we just do it yesterday? Why did I insist on making it all about her? My boner agrees.

As I reach her clit, I turn to face her. Should I touch her? What did 'no sex' actually mean? Her eyes are closed, her head resting on the edge of the bath.

"What the fuck are you waiting for?"

I laugh and slide my hand under her butt, lifting her out of the water. As my fingers glide down between her stubbly folds, my dick gives a little jolt, jealous of my hand. I have to be careful. I don't want to hurt her. Water is no lubricant. I rinse my hand, trace my finger around her pussy, gauging her reaction.

She bites her lip, and lets out a moan. I stroke her so lightly that I'm barely touching her, brushing against her skin. I sink my fingers deeper inside her, my thumb circling her clit.

She cries out, shakes beneath me, her pussy tightening on me then releasing.

Almost immediately she throws her hand to her head. *Shit.* She flies forward, cries out in pain, sending waves of water splashing over the side of the bath.

"My head." I lower my face to hers. She tilts her face, places her lips on mine, reassuring me. "I think, I think I need to get out, lie down for a while. Sorry. It was great. Sorry. Thank you."

"I'm so sorry, shit. Sorry." Damn it, sometimes my dick takes over my brain. I just can't with Caitlyn, I want her constantly.

"You didn't hurt me at all. It wasn't your fault." She laughs, but this is no laughing matter. What the hell was I thinking? I drain the water, gently rinse her off, then lift her out of the bath and dry her. Carrying her to the bedroom, I lay her on the bed then lie by her side. She snuggles up to me, running her fingers up and down my chest.

I ache for her, but I know better. Fighting the desire to roll on top of her, kiss her, make love to her. I've only been looking after her for half a day and I'm already doing a terrible job.

"You feeling better?"

She nods, smiles.

"I can call the doctor out, if you need me to."

"No, it's fine, really. The pain is subsiding. I think it was the rush of blood to the head."

"God, I really want to make love to you right now. You know that, right? But, I'm not going to do anything until you are one hundred percent well again."

"Hank, much as it *pains* me to say it, we should wait." She giggles at her pun. "Who knows what kind of injuries a woman with a concussion could sustain making whoopee with a man of your musculature, plus I'm not quite sure I could handle everything that's going on down here." She runs a solitary fingernail down the outside of my underwear, making me flinch.

"Kissing and stuff is okay, though, right?"

"Kissing and second base is just what the doctor ordered." She slides her hand down into my boxers and, not able to wait a second longer, I bury my head in those sumptuous breasts.

Chapter Twenty-Five

Caitlyn

Exactly one week after the wedding and the showdown with Hank's father, the doctor gives me the all-clear. The magazine has been closed down. The office is empty. Hanks owns the building, so my apartment is still there, but I've not wanted to leave his arms all week. Concussion is hard. Headaches, confusion. I have had a rough week.

I have things I need to say to Hank, but between getting his life in order, trying to talk to his family and looking after me, he's so tired and anxious. I've decided it can wait.

We've settled into a strange little routine over the last few days. Without any sexual shenanigans or work to occupy our time, we've been reading his vast collection of books, drinking tea and generally lounging around the pool. Hank is one of those people who has to be constantly occupied. Now that the house is finished, he's got itchy feet, and without a new project, he's spent most afternoons working out in the garden, lifting weights and making circuit training courses out of things he's found in his truck.

This morning, for example, he's doing something that involves crouching down on one knee and lifting a weight with his arm. I can't look away, the glistening sweat, the little grunts and the deep sighs, and that's just me.

I'm not sure the doctor would approve of me sitting under a lounger sipping tea and watching my hunky boyfriend lift weights in only a skimpy pair of shorts. It's doing very strange things to my heart rate.

He turns to see me staring and I pretend to delve back into my book. "Ted called. He wants to know if we're coming to Claire's birthday party this afternoon."

I look up, lower my sunglasses. "You told him about the magazine, right? I can't cover it."

"No, he's invited *us*."

"I thought your dad was going to make sure that your friends never speak to us again." I laugh, but it is tinged with anxiety. When I think back to that night in the hospital, how angry I made his father, how it could have ended so badly. I'm glad I stood up to him, but I realize now the danger I put myself in.

"I think my dad has illusions of grandeur far higher than his actual power over us. My friends' parents don't want to get involved in a family feud and we're all adults now. So do you want to go?"

"Will your family be there?"

He hesitates. "Yes."

"Well then, the question should actually be, *do you want to go*?"

He puts down his weight and sits back on the grass. "I have nothing to be ashamed of."

I smile. "I'm so proud of you. Standing up for yourself, doing what you want to do." I know how that feels. I know that coming here to America was a bold move on my part, but I don't regret a single second of it. "Well, it's decided then."

"Yup."

"We need a gift. Can you take me into town?"

"Caitlyn." I know what he's going to say. He's going to tell me to stop spending my money, that we have to be frugal now that neither of us has any income.

"I told you, I have savings. I don't mind. We're a partnership, right? I'm not a kept woman, I've been trying to tell you this for a while, but you and your billionaire family don't seem to understand the principle of 'real people' actually having a little cash in the bank."

"It makes me feel…impotent."

"Trust me. I can assure you that me spending money on you does not invalidate your masculinity in any way. Quite the contrary, there's nothing sexier than a kept man. Now drive me to town!" I click my fingers, and he bows.

"At your service, ma'am." His English accent is terrible, but I let it slide. I might treat myself to a new dress too, something to cheer me up. Maybe something more for Hank as well. He's been going on and on about a cordless drill, so I called a few people, bought him something nice. It'll be ready tomorrow. I cannot wait to give it to him. After a week of thoroughly pampering me, he deserves all the power tools in the world.

* * * *

I've yet to see Ted and Claire's house. It's as over the top as every other home I've visited in the last few weeks. No expense spared on the sweeping driveway, Roman columns and surrounding gardens. Hank's truck is now our only mode of transport and it sticks out like a sore thumb amongst the Bentleys and the Porsches.

I've opted for a long summer dress to cover up at least some of my bruises. They're at the black-to-yellowing phase. Plus the weather is still unusually warm and my pale skin, unaccustomed to more than three days of sun a year, is positively peeling. I'm glad I managed to bag a boyfriend before I turned into a week-old banana.

Claire, bless her, looks thoroughly miserable. She's at the *I don't want to do this anymore* stage of pregnancy and with her belly taking up most of her body, I can see why. I stride over, leaving Hank to catch up with his pals and hand her her gift.

"Hey, you. Don't get up." We give each other the regal wave I did at our first meeting. As much as I don't want her to get up, I don't want to bend down either. It's a win-win situation. I show her the gift and she points to a table piled high with hundreds of boxes.

"Thank you, anyway." She sits up, takes a sip of iced tea. "I missed you. How are you feeling?"

"Like shit on a stick," I reply, making her smile. "But it's getting better. What about you? Can you even walk anymore?"

"No. Ted is driving me absolutely mad and I haven't slept in days. It's too damned hot. Don't have a baby in summer." She rubs her belly. "I just want to meet him now, you know." Jen comes over to join us, gives me one of her famous hugs, causing me to wince quietly in pain, and sits down next to Claire.

"Can I get you guys anything to eat or drink?" I ask, salivating as I look over at the most magnificent display of food. I've been eating Hank's cooking for a week and I need something that isn't healthy. Zucchini isn't pasta, and cauliflower definitely isn't rice. I need to fill up on some carbs.

"Yes, please," says Claire, her eyes lighting up. Jen shakes her head.

I head over and grab a couple of plates.

"Hey, stranger," says a familiar voice behind me.

"Becky. How's married life treating you?" She holds up her wedding ring and plays with it, blinding me with the reflection of the sun.

"Awesome. Jonny is just the sweetest." She genuinely does look happy. Far more relaxed and frankly less bitchy than the first time I met her.

"Excuse me," says a voice from behind me. A hand pushes past my arm, and I turn to stare. "Well, hello there."

I gasp at him, loudly. Just for a second I think it's Guillermo. Same height, same portly shape, a few more hairs pulled across his head and a few years younger. "Oh, sorry," I say, as we do where I come from, even though he pushed me.

He doesn't reply. He just grabs a large shrimp from the edge of a silver bowl, dips it in sauce, sticks out his tongue and licks the sauce off before pushing the shrimp into his mouth. I assume this is supposed to be sexy in some way. This is his move.

I'm captivated and disgusted all at the very same time. He smiles at me and I nod and turn back to Becky, eyes wide. *What the hell?*

She winks at me. "It's okay. He's gone."

"Who, or what was that?"

"That," she replies, with a laugh, "was Baresi number two, Leo." I throw up in my mouth. No wonder I mistook him for his father. Two peas in a pod. "He really did get the short end of the stick, genetically." I'm glad she was the one to say it, I might have thought it, but never said it out loud.

I love Becky's frankness. Honestly, I didn't get it at first. She almost never has a nice word to say about anybody, but she's growing on me. "Yup."

"So tell me—" We're interrupted by a loud shout and both turn to see what the fuss is about.

It's me. I'm the fuss. It's happening and I can't do anything to stop it. And, of course, because karma hates me, the lads, minus Hank, are now sitting with Claire and Jen.

Everybody turns to stare.

"Lady DeVere. Lady DeVere! As I live and breathe." An English woman I don't know, drunk as the proverbial skunk, and wearing the most garish canary yellow suit and hat is standing a few feet away from me shouting, well, my name. I have about five seconds to come up with a plan. Run away? Hide under the buffet table?

I go for the *Me, you're talking to me?* plan, which involves pointing to oneself and looking rapidly left and right as if to confirm that they must be mistaken. But she's not having any of it.

She comes running over and takes my hand in hers. "My dear, it's been years. How are you? I heard about your grandmother, terrible shame." Her words are slurred, a slightly older gentleman in a suit is trying to drag her away from me. "Gerald, please, I'm talking to Lady DeVere."

He apologizes profusely and continues encouraging her to leave. Finally, coming to her senses, she calms down, and they make a rapid exit.

"Well, I think she's been on the gin," I say to Becky, my heart racing. I may just have got away with it. Everyone could clearly see how drunk she was. A case of mistaken identity can happen to anyone. But Becky isn't there anymore. She's running over to the others, phone in hand. *Shit. Shit, shit, shit.* "Becky, wait."

I run after her, but I'm too late. She's holding up her phone. Fuck, don't let it be Wikipedia. An article maybe, something simple, not the whole goddam description, estimated worth and, I can't even bear to think it, full title.

Jaws drop, phones come out and soon they're all sat there googling me. I stride over.

"Wow, what was that, eh?" I bite my top lip. I'm still going for mistaken identity, but it's too much too late. The minute you've got the name, you've got paparazzi photos, official photos and, um, the whole *royal* thing.

They all just look at me. Except for Chad, who jumps up and gets a selfie with me in the background. That'll be on every social media platform in seconds, with tags. He might be loyal to Hank and their group of friends, but he isn't going to show that loyalty to me.

Hank bounds up to the group, stands behind me, wrapping his hands tightly around my waist and grins. "What's going on? I just went for a whizz and someone said a drunk woman was shouting. What did I miss?"

Their attention turns from him, back to me, back to him. I shake my head. But this is too big. They're going to tell him. "Please, let me do it," I say, pleading with them.

I release Hank's hands from around my waist and loop my fingers through his. "Walk with me."

He laughs. "What's going on?"

I lead him through the garden toward the sea. "We need to talk about something."

"You keep saying that." *I know, and you keep putting it off. Or I do.*

"Yes, well, now I really need to tell you."

We arrive at a gangway that leads down to the sea, a bridge over the dunes. I lean on it and look out at sea.

"I'm going to talk, but you need to listen, please." My heart is beating so hard, he must be able to hear it. The pounding is so loud in my ears I can hardly think.

"I'm going to start by saying that I have never lied to you. It might seem like it, but I promise everything I've ever told you about my family, it's all true. I just kind of missed some bits out."

"Okay. Just don't tell me that my dad was right after all." He laughs, but I don't join him.

"Oh, your dad? He's going to love this story."

"What?"

I take the deepest breath I've ever taken in my life. "My name is Caitlyn Walsh. When my parents divorced, I took my mother's name. It was just easier, for so many reasons. She was very well-meaning, my mum. She had a slightly different outlook on life than most people and I think that's what drew my dad to her. They got married in a commune, in Ireland of all places. I spent the first couple of years of my life there until my parents divorced."

"So far, so good."

"Look… You have to see this from my point of view. I didn't see my father from the moment he left my mum until her funeral ten years later. I spent almost every summer, at least two or three weeks, with my grandmother. She was an amazing woman. Incredible. Kind and loving and she doted on me. I lived with her until I was sixteen, but I'd never been to school and couldn't envisage university, so I got a job as a secretary, moved out and did my own thing."

Hank puts his hands on the bridge, leans back on to it. "Where is this leading, exactly?"

"I'm trying to give you context for the next bit."

"Is it bad?" He looks worried. He knows it can't be good or we wouldn't be doing this here, now.

"No. I just should have told you sooner. I tried to, at the wedding, when you said you loved me and at the hospital, but I swear every time, something or someone interrupted me. Then it just sort of felt like I'd gone too far. I didn't know how you'd react."

"You know you can tell me anything, right?" He steps forward, but I step back. I need to be standing tall when I tell him this, not safe in his trusting arms. I don't deserve it.

"I know, but this is big." I take another deep breath. "So, my grandmother, appalled by my father's behavior, especially concerning me, disinherited him about seven years ago. He was her only child and I'm his only child. Which means that I inherited everything when she passed."

"I get it. So what, you've got a bit of money, a house in the UK, that sort of thing."

I close my eyes, take another deep breath. "Yeah, something like that."

"God, Caitlyn, just tell me." A line etches between his brows as his eyes narrow and a solitary bead of sweat rolls down my back. This is Hank, I can tell him everything and it will all be okay. Because he loves me.

"My official title is Lady Caitlyn of Becestershire, my grandfather having been Lord Henry of Becestershire. My other title, which is less used, but as valid, is Her Royal Highness, Princess Caitlyn of Mendava." I explain how the country was dissolved, way before my birth, but the title remains. He doesn't say anything, just stares at me, mouth gaping open. "It's just words. It isn't me."

"Princess. Like an actual princess with a crown? You mean you weren't joking when you said..." People always love the crown thing. I don't have crown hair. They just float, five inches above my head.

"A tiara. But it's in a bank vault. It's not like I carry the crown jewels around with me." I laugh, but Hank just looks at me. He's hurting and I get it. I'm not the person he fell in love with. Well, I am and yet, I'm not at the same time.

I scrunch my nose up. "There's something else."

"Another title?" He uses a mocking tone, it's hard to tell if he's serious or not.

"I'm rich. Like, you know how most of you are rich and then Ted's family is like *rich*, rich. I fall into the *rich*, rich category. In fact, ironically, I'm probably worth more than your father." I stop talking and wait for Hank to take it all in.

He looks me dead in the eyes. "So you lied to me."

"No. I never lied. I just didn't tell you everything." Not technically lying, but not truthful either. "I only found out about the extent of the money and all the titles when my grandmother died. This is all new to me too."

"Being dishonest and hiding shit like this is lying, Cait."

I rub my palms together and ramble on, hoping that something will click with him, that he'll see my side. "I knew I was the queen's third cousin removed or something, but I didn't know the rest. I thought all the money would go to my father."

"The Queen...*of England*, that queen." Fuck. Yes, *that* queen.

"It's not important, and it doesn't change who I am. I'm still Caitlyn. I'm still just a girl who wants to read books and write articles and take photographs."

"But you lied to me. I was in love with you. I told you I loved you." He strides back and forth, back and forth, rubbing his forehead.

I stand in front of him, grab his forearms, but he rips them away. "You *were* in love with me? Nothing's changed. I'm still me." I need him to understand, to see why I did this. He knows what it's like to be pressured into being something you're not. He gets me, even if he doesn't realize it.

He walks away again, turns his back on me, then comes storming back. "No secrets. That's what we said. I was willing to give up my family and my friends for you and you lied to me."

"I was in too deep. You get that, right? I was supposed to come here, live in an apartment and work for a magazine. None of this was supposed to happen. I just wanted to be the journalist I'd worked so hard to be. I wanted to take photos of local events and write articles about churches and wineries. I couldn't do any of that if you all knew who I was."

"Why?" If only he knew the millions of times I've asked myself that very question. Every cutting remark from Becky. Every time I've been treated like a second-class citizen. I am that person, though. I'm not the title. I'm just Caitlyn.

"I'm supposed to have a security detail, chauffeurs, advisors. You know what it's like. You live in this world too. Kidnapping, robbery. Then there's the paparazzi. This is not the life I was brought up in. In fact, up until this year, it wasn't even a life I knew I was going to have." *See my point of view. Understand.*

Hank is running his hands through his hair, striding backward and forward, his face getting redder and redder. I've never seen him so angry.

I'm frantic. I'm losing him. All my fears about telling him the truth are coming true, and I can't do anything about it. I try to grab his arm again, to make some kind of physical contact. I need his warmth, his protection. He makes me feel safe and I need that now more than ever.

"But you could have told *me*, right? What were you going to do, just pretend for the rest of your life that you aren't the Princess of fucking Switzerland?"

"Mendava," I say. Tears well up in my eyes. I drop my arms, stop trying to make him stay. He's going to leave me. "But it's just a title on a piece of paper."

"Were you just going to let us live off of beans and rice when you've got enough money in the bank to buy the whole fucking island?"

"I told you I had savings. We haven't gone without. I saw something in you. Kindred spirits, remember? I saw the same person." Somebody from privilege, who could have gone into the family business, but instead, chose to do what made them happy. "That's what made me fall in love with you. You're just like me. I was going to tell you... I tried."

"But what? What happened? Why are you telling me now?"

"Somebody recognized me and then everybody looked me up on the internet and now they all know." I look back at the party. Have I lost all of my friends too? "I'm...uh...I'm kind of a big deal. They made this stupid list of eligible princesses or something and it went viral. I didn't know what to do, I didn't have any family to talk to and my friends all sort of got a bit weird about it. Then one of my tutors told me about this job that he'd recommended me for, and here I am."

"I need time to think about this."

"No, don't go please, Hank. We can talk about this, work it out, right? We love each other, don't we? Please. just listen to me."

"People who love each other don't lie. How can I believe anything you say ever again? You deceived us all. I gave up my family for you. Do you even get that? You're a selfish little..." He lets the sentence drop.

Wow. Okay. I let my head drop. Take a second to reply.

He starts to walk back toward the party. "Hank, please."

"No, Caitlyn. Just don't." I want to let him go, admit defeat, but I just can't.

I run in front of him and put my arms out to stop him, but he pushes me away. "You still love me, right?" I watch him as he walks away from me. "Hank?"

"How can I love somebody I don't even know?"

He is gone. I knew this moment would come, but I thought I'd have some control over it, ease him into it. I allow myself to fall to the ground, to give up. My whole body hurts. The bruises will heal, but my heart is ripping in two.

I wait a while then walk back through the party, head down. I don't say a word to anybody, just keep going. Hank is gone. He must have left straight away. I don't even have a ride. This rich little princess is going to have to call a cab or walk home. Claire and Ted's house isn't in one of the private lanes that exist on the island for rich families. Paparazzi are waiting, cameras at the ready, outside of their home.

It's not for me. There are quite a few well-known names on the guest list. It doesn't mean that they aren't waiting for me now though. Chad's online posts have probably made the rounds by now. People know I'm here.

Two or three of them follow me, calling out 'Princess' and 'Lady DeVere' as they chase me down the street. Tears are flooding down my face. I'm ugly crying in the street and all these people want is a photo of it. Is it so bad that I don't even care anymore? They can stick shots of my snotty tear-ridden face on all the gossip sites, it's of no matter to me.

A car draws up beside me. Ted. "Let me take you home. It's the least I can do." He's a good friend. I settle in beside him. "He'll cool down. Don't worry."

I wipe my face with my arm. He whips a cotton handkerchief from his top pocket and hands it to me. Ted is going to be an awesome dad. "I ruined everything."

"I'm sure you had your reasons." He smiles at me. "You know, I don't think I've ever seen Hank as happy as he has been with you. He'll come around."

"No. He's so mad at me. His family aren't speaking to him because of me. All I had to do was tell the truth and they would have welcomed me with open arms. I should never have let it get this far. I needed time to get my mind around it myself before I could talk about it. I don't want to be that person. I want to be Caitlyn. I'm sorry. I'm boring you." All I do is ramble. Why can't I just shut my damned mouth?

"Not at all. That's what friends are for."

"I want to go home, get away from here. I've fucked everything up." I look up, embarrassed by my language in front of Ted, but he doesn't even flinch.

"Hank's house, the apartment?"

I shake my head. "No, *home*, home." I deceived Hank. He was very clear that he doesn't love me. I came here to do a job, and that doesn't even exist anymore. Plus, my cover's blown. I'll get no peace now. Time to quit before this gets any worse.

Chapter Twenty-Six

Hank

I was so mad yesterday that I walked clean out of the party, took my truck and just drove. Princess Caitlyn. The girl I was going to marry. She's lied to me since the beginning. Lied about our hook-up on the plane, then lied about who she was, about having any money. No wonder she kept getting pissed off at us for buying her clothes. They probably aren't even good enough for her royal ass.

Ted is fucking annoying me, hopping from one foot to another. "Shall we go?"

"What is this?"

"Let's just go," says Jonny. He twirls his car key around his finger. "Get it over with."

"You got somewhere to be?" I ask him. They're the ones who woke me up this morning, dragged me out of bed. I would much rather be sleeping off the three-quarters of a bottle of whiskey that got me to sleep last night than standing here now.

We drive maybe twenty minutes then draw up at a simple brick building. Nice renovation. They've recently replaced the awning instead of painting it, which is always a sign of a job well done.

Ted opens the door.

The room is old, a bit musty, about thirty-feet square. To the left is an architect's table, with an antique desk lamp over it, a box of business cards sitting on top. I pick one up. It's got my number on it and *Baresi Renovations. Fuck. What is this place?*

All along the back wall is a grill with hooks on it, tools hanging down. I wander around the room, inspecting, exploring. The drill I mentioned the other week, the table saw. Everything I've always wanted. "Cait did this? When?"

"She started planning it when you got together. As a surprise. Honestly, man, we had no clue. She just told us, before she left, to bring you here this morning and give you the keys."

There are a couple of worktables with vises and along the right-hand side, shelves and units with little compartments for screws and nails. I opened them. It's perfect, right down to the very finest detail. Little Miss Post-it Note has been very thorough here.

I think back to when she said that my head massage was better than sex and I get it now. I'm getting off on drills and workbenches. She'll laugh when she hears it.

Except she won't.

Because I'm a stupid fucking idiot who doesn't know what he's got until it's gone. "Where is she? I want to speak to her."

"She's gone," says Ted.

"What do you mean? Gone where?"

"Home. I arranged for my car to take her early this morning." He shrugs his shoulders. He's mad at me for not listening, for walking away. Ted and I have been friends forever and I know when I've disappointed him.

It's not the first time. When I dropped out of college, I took my inheritance and split. I never even said goodbye and that hurt him and the other guys. Nobody even knew where I was. I can't deal with confrontation, I hate it. I have to go away and think about things. He's not said it, but I know him and I know he thinks I'm a jerk for leaving Caitlyn yesterday and he's right.

"Why?"

"Because somebody took a photo of her, tagged her in it and then put it all over the internet." Ted throws daggers at Chad. "You know the paps followed her down the street, right? She was on her own, and it was fucking dangerous."

"What? No." Why hadn't they called me? *Because I'd switched my phone off.*

Ted turns to me. "She left because someone broke her heart, because he wasn't man enough to listen to her, understand what she had to say." *Fuck.* Ted is really pissed with me, and he has every right to be.

"But there's a chance that she hasn't actually gone yet, right? I mean, maybe her flight's later today."

"This isn't what she wants," replies Ted. "She was pretty cut up last night, wanted to go back to England. She didn't feel safe here anymore." Yesterday, when we'd argued, she kept grabbing my arms. She just wanted to feel protected.

"I was so angry." I struggle to say it. "I told her I didn't love her. I didn't mean it. I was just in shock."

Honestly, it's a bit of a blur. I know I said some pretty nasty shit, but I was completely taken aback.

"Man, that's no excuse. If you love her you have to take the good with the bad."

"Take me to the airport, please. I need to make this better. I have to find her, explain to her that I was wrong." Even if it meant flying across an ocean.

"You really love her, huh?" asks Chad.

"Yes." He and I were going to have strong words about his part in this, but it would have to wait.

"Well, then, let's go get your girl," says Jonny.

We jump into Jonny's car. The first and only time I've ever thanked the Lord for Jonny's need for speed. I belong to the only billionaire's club where three out of four members drive sensible cars.

An hour and a half is a long time to wait to see if someone has caught a plane. While my friends sing along to Jonny's playlist, I mull over the events of the last few weeks.

I'm mad. Mad at Cait because she lied, mad at my family, mad at everyone. But I do love her. She was right. She is the only person I've ever met who has truly got me. Believed in me.

That's all she was asking of me, to see the person and not the princess.

And I walked away. I'm a fucking dumbass sometimes.

Chapter Twenty-Seven

Caitlyn

Delays and cancelations. I need to get away from here before I change my bloody mind and all I've encountered are delays and cancelations. My flight is going to leave four hours late. No money in the world will get that flight to leave on time.

"You again." The old lady with the son in Manhattan. She looks chirpier, a lot less uptight than the outgoing flight.

"Isn't this a funny old coincidence?" Isn't she only supposed to be staying a couple of weeks? How long have I been in America? "Shouldn't you have gone back to the UK by now?"

She shrugs her shoulders. "Weren't you moving here?"

"Yes." I don't want to go. I've made friends here, started to feel like I had a place amongst the people of Sag Harbor.

She smiles at me. "Well, I met a very nice gentleman, decided to stay a bit longer."

I chuckle. The irony. "I met one too. That's why I'm leaving."

She places a hand on my arm, just as my grandmother would have done. This old lady's kindness makes me feel a million times more alone. "Did he break your heart, dear?"

"No. I may have broken his though, and his family didn't approve."

"Oh no, well that's the way sometimes, isn't it? Could have been worse. You could have ended up with that young man from the plane over. Remember him? I told my Harry about it and he thought it was hilarious. These Americans, so much more relaxed when it comes to things of a sexual nature." So that's why she is so chirpy. I don't have the courage to tell her that it is, indeed, the guy from the plane. The way this conversation is going, she'll be congratulating me on finding such a well-hung lover.

"So was it just a holiday romance, with your gentlemen?" I ask. I'd much rather talk about her guy than mine.

"Oh no, dear, quite the opposite. He asked me to marry him. Can you imagine? I suppose, when you get to our age, you do these things quicker. I'm going home to get my affairs in order and then I'll be on the next available flight back. Harry says I can live in his condo. What an odd word. I kept calling it a maisonette. He found that ever so funny."

"Oh, well" — I choke back the need to cry — "that's nice for you." Nope. I'm going to cry.

She wraps her arms around me and rubs my back. "Oh, my poor love. You *did* get your heart broken, didn't you? Is there really nothing you can do? Will your young man take you back?"

"It's complicated." That's the least you could say about this situation.

She squeezes my arm. "These things have a way of working themselves out, you know." I'm starting to get attached to this sweet old lady. I might have to keep her.

I let out a regretful sigh. "It's too late now, anyway."

"Saying goodbye is hard."

I turn to look at her, allowing the tears to stream down my cheeks. "I never said goodbye." I ran away. That's the truth of the matter. When things get hard, I run away.

"What? Oh my word, dear, does he not know you did this? Oh, you have to tell him you're leaving, let him say goodbye. Otherwise you'll both always wonder."

"It's too hard." It is. I can't do it, I'll crack when I see that beautiful face of his and he doesn't want me anymore. Not the real me.

"Oh, love, you are in a pickle. It's not too late, you know. You can turn around now, go and talk to him. You'll regret it if you don't. My son wasn't too keen when I met Harry, but I told him he just had to lump it. It'll work out, you'll see, if it's meant to be."

She's right. I need to talk to Hank. I'll always regret it if I don't. "I don't know if I can."

She smiles at me. "You won't know if you don't try, will you?"

I grab my stuff. "I'm doing it."

She hugs me, again. God, I love this woman who I don't even know. "Good for you."

I leap to my feet and head for the exit. "Have a great flight. Maybe I'll see you and Harry around New York sometime."

* * * *

How the hell do you get out of an airport? It takes ten minutes of persuasion with the TSA officer to let me back through security. Apparently *for love* isn't a good enough reason for disrupting the system. I'm not ashamed to say it. I throw the Baresi name out there and it works.

I'm back in New York, with only a backpack to keep me company and a simple plan. Find Hank, explain everything and say goodbye.

Jen isn't answering her phone, so I call Claire. She insists on sending a car, says that I can take a cab to Long Island.

Forty-five minutes later and my transport arrives, with Claire inside.

"I decided to come too. I can't drive, but I'm so bored. This baby is never going to come out of my body, so if I'm going to have to spend the rest of my life looking like an elephant I might as well leave the house occasionally."

I'm not sure that that was a good idea, but I'm not one to argue with a heavily pregnant woman. "Thank you so much for picking me up."

"What's the plan? Are you going to run back into Hank's open arms?"

"No. I'm going to say goodbye. And I'm going to talk to him. I was wrong to leave like I did. It was the coward's way out. We need to talk about what happened."

"So you're not ruling anything out, right? Because that guy loves you. You know that he'd do anything for you."

"He told me he doesn't, that he doesn't even know me."

"Bullshit. Aaah!" She winced in pain. "That man loves you and he has never loved any other woman in his life. You can see it a mile away."

"Are you okay?" She nods and signals for me to carry on while doubled over in pain. "But his family, what about them?"

"Ah, they'll get…aah, over it, aah! Once they find out who you are, they'll…ah…they'll never leave you alone." She has a point, but that is exactly why I didn't tell anybody who I was in the first place. I wanted people to like me for me.

Nobody that heavily pregnant and grabbing my hand as if she is trying to squeeze the life out of it is '*okay*'. "Claire, are you in labor?" *Shit. Please say no. I can't do this right now.*

"Braxton…aaah…Hicks. Had them for a while now. Oh, oh no. No, my water just broke. No, I'm in labor."

Holy fucking crap shit. What?

I start googling childbirth. "Where do we…what do we do?"

Liquid—I hesitate to say water because let's be honest, that does not smell like something that came out of a tap—has seeped all over the lovely leather seats and is dripping onto the floor.

She leans forward and places a hand on the driver's shoulder. "Ken, please take us to Gacilly Hospital, and make it fast."

"Yes, ma'am."

"I need Ted. You need to get hold of Ted." She's stretched out now, back against the door, legs akimbo. Despite the swollen ankle blocking my view, I grab my phone, but I'm out of battery. "Shit."

She rips it out of my hand and hands it to Ken. "Charge this." Then she hands me hers.

There's no answer from Ted so I text, then call again.

Chapter Twenty-Eight

Hank

By the time we've gotten to the airport we've ascertained, using our amazing private detective skills that Caitlyn is still in New York. Her phone had gone dead about ten minutes ago, but up until that point, she'd still been here.

"I hope it doesn't mean she's gone."

"You can't know for sure until we check flights."

"Which terminal do we want? Shit, there's like a dozen of them."

"Wait, my guy dropped her off at terminal seven, I remember."

"Awesome." With three men guiding Jonny, it only takes us two trips to terminal four and a couple of wrong turns toward arrivals before we get to terminal seven.

"Get out, and go get her. We'll park."

"I'm coming with you," says Ted.

The two of us leap out of the car and run like hell to security.

Then we stop.

Shit, there's no way we're getting past TSA. We can't even buy a ticket just to get past them, and neither of us has thought to bring a passport.

"Holy fucking crappy shit."

A portly TSA officer bars our way. He looks pissed, like *arresting people* pissed. "Sir, can I help you?"

I hold up my hands. "I need to get through there. It's my girlfriend, I have to get her back..." He rolls his eyes, sighs and lets go of his gun holster.

"What is it with you people today? Don't tell me, *it's for love?*" He lets out a mocking laugh and rolls his eyes again.

"Yes." What else can I do? I crane my neck to see if I can spot her.

He bars our way once again, his tone more serious this time. "Sir, please, don't do that. I'm going to have to ask you to back away."

Ted steps in. "Officer, is there any way you could let us through? This is Hank Baresi, son of Guillermo Baresi..."

"Look, man, I don't care if he's the Pope, this ain't Disneyland, okay? You have a ticket you go in. You don't have a ticket, you don't go in. Wait...did you say Baresi?"

"Yes, why?" A glimmer of hope. Finally, my name is actually going to be useful to me other than getting into a club or a bar.

"I think I can help you. I let a British girl out, pretty blonde with all the curves, insisted she had to go back 'for love', and mentioned your name."

We've missed her by half an hour. I hug the TSA guy, who is not amused and stinks of baloney, and run back to the car.

"I'll call Jonny," says Ted. "Wait. Shit, shit, shit, shit. There's like a million messages from Claire. Hank, I'm going to be a daddy."

"Ted, Claire's twice the size of Manhattan. We *know* that you're going to be a daddy."

"No. Hey! Zip it. That's my wife. No, I'm going to be a daddy, like today."

What the fuck? Crap, and I'd dragged him to New York with me.

"Tell her to cross her legs." I call Jonny myself. "Man, you need to get here now. We've got an emergency."

Chapter Twenty-Nine

Caitlyn

"You need to breathe. What did they teach you in Lamaze?"

"Fuck that, I need drugs."

"I have paracetamol." If looks could kill, I'll be embalmed and buried before dusk. "Can't we try the doggy breathing thing or something, like in films?"

"Caitlyn, a human person is pushing his way out of me. Breathing will not help. Aaah!"

Claire is full-on in the birthing position and I have the worst view. Her legs are now straddling my shoulders and she's grabbing both of my hands and breaking every bone in my fingers.

"We need to time them, don't we?"

"Yes." The sound of AC/DC rocks out of her phone. "It's Ted. Pick up."

"You're going to have to loosen your death grip for me to do that." She releases one of my hands, and I pick up.

"Hey, honey, how are you doing?" Ted sounds remarkably calm.

"It's Caitlyn. I'll put you on speaker."

"Ted! My water broke. We're on our way back from JFK." She lets out a mild scream then resumes talking, with a slightly more gravelly, slightly more possessed voice. "You need to get your ass to the hospital."

"I will, I'm…uh… We're at JFK."

"What the fuck?" Oh, she is *definitely* possessed.

"We, uh… Look… It's complicated. Jonny's here. He's going to take me straight to the hospital. I'll be there as soon as I can. Uh, should I pass the phone over to Hank?"

I shake my head, but it's too late.

Hank's voice comes out of the speaker. "Cait, don't leave. I need to talk to you. I was an idiot. Forgive me."

"Hank, I can't do this now, but you were right. I haven't been honest. I'm sorry. But it's too late, I've messed everything up. I'm sorry." I hang up the phone and put it on timer.

Claire looks me in the eyes. "He loves you, you know. Don't give up on him."

"I don't deserve him. I fucked up." She shakes her head at me. I'm not worthy of this sweet man, who is still prepared to take me back, even though I lied through my teeth for an entire month. I don't want to talk about this. I feel shit enough as it is. "Do we time the contractions or in between them?"

"How the fuck do I know? That was Ted's only job."

Okay.

"Both," says Ken, from the front of the car. "You need to time from the moment her belly tightens to when it relaxes and then you need to time in between each contraction. From what I've heard, we're good. You haven't even really started yet."

We're good? This is going to get worse? I don't think my hands can take it.

"Thank you, Ken." I mean it. What a lifesaver. I definitely need my own driver.

"Your friend is right, though, ma'am. You need to breathe through the contractions."

Claire starts to well up. "No, no, no, don't cry. We can do this, right?" I Google Lamaze breathing and explain it to Claire. Hopefully, it's going to help with the fact that right now she looks homicidal. The next contraction comes. I time it, and she breathes, and the tension in the car releases just a little.

"How long, Ken?"

"About forty minutes, traffic allowing."

I look over to Claire, her eyes narrow and the tension goes right back up to that which you could cut with a knife. Crap.

"So really, why did you go?"

I look over to Ken. Should I be discussing this in front of him? "Because Hank doesn't love me anymore, I have no job and his family aren't even speaking to him because of me."

Claire's face turned from a pained scowl to an angry one. "His family aren't speaking to him because they're dumbasses. It shouldn't matter whether or not you're the Queen of France." I want to correct her, but I can feel the room, and being pedantic isn't going to cut it right now.

Chapter Thirty

Hank

"So Caitlyn is in your car," says Chad.

"Uh-huh." Ted is as white as a sheet.

"And Claire is with her and she's giving birth?" asks Jonny. Ted pales even further.

"In labor," I replied. "Not giving birth. Plenty of time. Claire just texted me."

"Claire doesn't have her phone. Caitlyn texted you." Caitlyn is on the other end of the phone. "I see you, Enrico Baresi. Don't text her. She's helping my wife."

I put down my phone. "Do you want to put some music on or something?" I ask Jonny. Both Ted and I need some thinking time.

Caitlyn has changed her mind. Is she coming back? The TSA guy had mentioned something about her wanting to come back *for love*. I'm still mad as hell at her for going, but at the same time I just wanted to squash her in my arms and kiss her and do dirty things with her until she screams.

Ted turns to look at me. "What are you going to do?"

"About Cait?" I have no fucking idea.

"No, about the plastic in the oceans. Of course I meant about Caitlyn."

I stare down at my feet. "I'll do whatever it takes to win her back—move to her castle or wherever princesses live."

He tips his head to the side. "So you forgive her for lying?"

"I guess. She had her reasons and I need to understand that. All this depends on why she came back."

"She loves you, Hank. That's all you need to know."

The urge to be with her, to hold her, is so strong. I just want to get there. "All I want is her. Nothing else matters. Nothing."

He raises his hands and punches me on the arm. "Well then, you have to fight for her, tell her how you feel. You kids tire me out with your relationship shit. Just communicate, for fuck's sake."

I rub my arm. He's mean when he's trying to prove a point. "You kids? You're younger than me."

"By a couple of months, but relationship-wise I'm like your grandfather." He shakes his head, and we go back to looking out of the window. He's right though. I need to get her back.

Chapter Thirty-One

Caitlyn

"What is taking so long?" I say it through my teeth, in the hopes that Claire won't hear it over her contraction breathing.

"Traffic," says Ken, looking over his shoulder as we sit, patiently waiting to move forward another inch.

"The contractions are every three minutes and they're really long. What does that mean?" I have internet access. I know what that means, I just need Ken's reassurance that we'll make it in time.

"It means I'm pulling over and calling an ambulance. That baby is coming now." He drives us into a rest area and jumps out of the car, phone in hand.

Jonny's car screeches to a halt next to us and the four musketeers pile out. Looks like Chad is back in favor again.

The door cracks open behind Claire, and she grabs the seat to steady herself.

Ted. Oh thank Christ," I say.

He slips in behind her. The front doors open and Hank, Chad and Jonny join the fray. "Guys, too many people in the delivery room here." Jonny and Chad back out.

Hank places a hand on my back. "Can we talk?"

"You're kidding, right? I'm kind of busy here." I look up at Ted and Claire, but they signal to me to listen to what he has to say. Claire starts to contract again. "You have thirty seconds." I start timing.

"I'm sorry for the way I reacted. You didn't deserve it. I should have talked it out, listened to you. I was wrong."

I stare at the timer, avoiding his gaze. Claire's contractions are getting longer and longer. "I'm sorry I lied. I had my reasons, but you didn't deserve…one minute sixteen seconds." I turn to look at him. "I should have told you."

"I was so mean yesterday, so angry. I'm sorry." I look back at Claire and Ted, their hands entwined.

Claire nods at me through her deep breaths. I can't believe I'm multitasking childbirth and working out my problems with my boyfriend.

"I came back because I want you to know that I love you, I wanted you to hear it one last time from me. You deserve to find a woman who loves you for you. And I need the same, someone who loves me for me — not the lady or the princess, but the journalist, the avid reader, the tea drinker."

Hank gets up on his knees, leans over the seat and places a hand on the back of my head. "But I do, I do love you. None of it matters if you're not here." He's looking the other way, avoiding whatever's going on between Claire's legs, but he lays his forehead on me.

"No, I lied to you." Another contraction. Already? Fuck, it's getting close. "All my life I've wanted a family, and I denied you of yours. You have every right to be angry."

Claire lets out a low howl. This is a big one. I rub my hands around her belly. I have no idea if it's helping, but I've got to do something.

"You didn't do anything. They did. Don't go, Cait, I can't bear it without you."

"It's getting closer, Claire. We need to get ready for this little guy." I turn back to Hank. "Why don't you hate me? For running away."

"Never. I could never hate you." He shakes his head and smiles at me. "I love you. And you came back to me."

I put down the phone. It's almost time. I approach Hank's face. "What if you regret it. What if—" I brush my lips close to his. I want to kiss him so badly, just got this baby to deliver then I'm going to devour this man.

"No. No regrets. The moment I knew for sure that I loved you, I knew that I was giving them up. I don't care anymore. I need you in my life."

Claire grabs my hand. "Caitlyn, stop making out with Hank. I feel like I need to push." *Shit, I can't do this.* I turn my full attention back to her lady parts.

"Claire, I don't know what I'm doing here. You need to hold that baby in…" She glares at me with the power of a thousand swords. I swear, her eyes turn red. "Or don't, whatever feels best. Guys, do we have any towels, warm water, a midwife?"

Ted looks at me, eyes wide. "There's a picnic blanket in the trunk."

"God, I have to do everything." I rip open my backpack. I have spare clothes, I'll use them. I lay out my T-shirt and my sweatpants. They'll have to do. "Claire, I'm going to remove your panties. Ted, any chance they taught you how to deliver a baby at law school? Ted?" He's white as a sheet. I throw him my sternest look. "Don't you pass out on me."

Claire lets out a guttural roar. I rip off her underwear and bend closer to have a look.

It's red and swollen and icky. Is that good? Biology was never my forte at school.

"What can you see?"

"A vagina." *What am I supposed to see?*

"You're supposed to see if the cervix is dilated," says Ted. I'm pretty sure it's quite dilated by now. "You have to put your hand in, like the doctor."

I look at Claire. "Okay, I'm going in." Hank makes a heaving noise and hides back behind the front seat. My fingers only don't find a cervix, they find a tuft of baby hair. "Oh my God, I can feel his head." Don't panic. Breathe.

She starts to weep. "I can't do it. I can't. I need a doctor. I need drugs."

I place my hands on her belly. "We don't have any choice. This guy is coming out now. I am right here for you. We can do this, together. Women give birth to babies all around the world, every day. We've got this." Her stomach tightens. "Push, Claire, push with everything you've got." She roars once more. You have to give it to her, for such a tiny person, Claire's a warrior.

The top of a head appears. "I can see hair. Oh my God, you're doing it. Take a deep breath, get ready, just a couple more pushes." *Oh shit. I'm delivering a baby. A real-life baby.*

She's breathless, scared. "I can't."

"You can, I can see his little tiny head. You've got this." There isn't a dry eye in this car. Or a relaxed muscle. The tension is at boiling point. I cannot fuck this up.

Ted hugs his wife, coming to his senses. "I'm here, baby. We've got this."

Her stomach tightens. "Push!" I shout. The head comes out. "Wait!" The cord is around his little neck. *Shit, shit, shit.* My hands are shaking, but I need to stay calm.

"What? What is it?" Ted's panicking. He can see what I'm doing, but I give him my best *shut the fuck up* look and carry on. I slip my finger under the cord, stretching it out. "Everything is *fine*. Last push and we're done, guys."

I catch Ted and Claire's tiny little baby boy in my Muppets T-shirt, unravel the cord, tap his little feeties until he cries then place him on her chest.

"It's a baby. Oh my God, you delivered a baby." Hank is staring wide-eyed at me like I've just invented penicillin.

"I suppose I did. Well, Claire did most of the work."

She looks over to me, smiling from ear to ear. "Thank you, I can never thank you enough."

"Oh, stop it. You did it all. You were amazing. Occasionally terrifying, but look at what you did. You made a tiny human."

Chapter Thirty-Two

Caitlyn

The paramedics draw up and take control of the situation. I'm in a state. My clothes are covered in fluids and gunk. It isn't a great look.

"Want to hitch a ride back with us?" asks Hank.

Jonny looks me up and down and shakes his head. "Nah, I don't think so." There is no way I'm getting in his precious car. Ken announces that he's called a car for us, should be here in fifteen minutes.

Everyone leaves one by one until Hank and I are left standing there just looking at each other, in awe of what just happened, reeling from the events of the past few days.

"I love you," I say, taking his hand in mine.

"Me too," he says. "We need to talk. You bought me a workshop."

"If a princess can run a magazine, a billionaire can renovate houses." The minute I met him, it seemed like fate was drawing us together and it took me a minute to work out why. We needed each other. "I bought your house too."

"What?"

"I'm sorry. When we stayed there last week, it felt so...right." I look down. "I wanted to spend the rest of my life lying in bed with you looking at the stars. It was all part of this big surprise I was planning, but I...uh...everything just got really complicated."

"Don't you have an observatory in your castle, or whatever?"

My castle? "I don't have a castle. My grandmother left me a small apartment in Mayfair. The rest of my properties are tied up in charitable foundations."

"Properties?" he replies, looking confused. I look at my feet and reply under my breath. "What? I can't hear you." *That's because I don't want you to hear me.*

"Twenty-two properties." I cringe. It sounds worse than it is.

"Cool. Okay, what else should I know while we're at it?" We sit down on the grass verge.

"There's the family jewels." I slide my hand up his thigh. "Although I prefer yours." I'm so horny for this guy right now. I definitely need a shower first, though.

He pulls me onto his lap. "And?"

"That's it, the titles, the properties, the stupid, unnecessarily large amount of money."

He places his mouth on mine. My toes curl, my body melts into his and my heart heals. How can I even have considered walking away from this man?

A car draws up. "Looks like that's our ride," says Hank, placing his hand in mine and heaving us to our feet. "Shall we go home, princess?"

Home. I guess this place is home now. It's going to be complicated, but we have friends here, and maybe some family.

I'm right where I want to be, in Hank's arms. Just like fate intended.

Chapter Thirty-Three

Caitlyn

The car takes us back to the house, and after a shower and a little family jewel inspection, we both have a well-deserved nap.

A few hours later, a steaming mug of tea is wafted under my nose. "Cait?"

"Mmm, thank you." I stir with difficulty, needing at least eight or so more hours sleep. "I'm awake." I shake my head. "I'm awake."

Hank is standing over me, looking more than awake and ready to do something that doesn't involve staying under this nice warm quilt.

"If you're not too tired, I'd like to take you somewhere this evening, just the two of us. It's one of my favorite places. I've wanted to take you there for a while." He looks way too excited for me to complain and drag him under the covers, so I acquiesce.

We pile into his truck and up the coast to his favorite beach. Sandwiches, a pile of blankets to sit on and a decent bottle of wine are neatly packed in a picnic hamper. He's thought of everything.

"I love you," I say as I gaze at his handsome face, making him laugh and push me away. I'm so enamored with this man right now. Totally and utterly under his charm.

The place is deserted. It's a pebbled beach, which is probably the reason why it's so empty, but the sun is setting and it's ideal for a late evening picnic.

"When I was a kid, Poppa, my grandfather, would bring me here to fish. He was a good man you know, not like my dad, ruthlessly ruled over by Nonna. He worked right up until he died. I don't think he ever took time off, except when he brought me here."

"It's beautiful." This is so calming, especially after the last few days. Peaceful. Exactly what we need.

"I've always come here when I had a decision to take or a heart to break." He picks up a pebble, and throws it into the sea. "And when I need to contemplate my next move."

I cringe. "That sounds ominous."

He laughs and shakes his head. "Don't worry. That's not why I brought you here. Poppa used to say that if you write a wish on a pebble and throw it into the sea, it would settle back one day with the tide and your wish would come true. Of course, I was more of a romantic back then." He smiles at me.

"You're not a romantic anymore?"

His eyes squint as he reflects on his reply. "I lost track of who I was. Got caught up in being the life of the party, then I went traveling, then lost myself in my renovations. I don't know, am I?"

"Yes, of course you are. You're not a flowers-and-chocolate guy, but looking at the stars or having my back scrubbed by you? That's pretty romantic. This isn't bad either." I serve us both a glass of wine.

He puts his arm around my shoulders and pulls me into him, kissing the top of my head. "A month ago you came into my life, blew me away. I never thought I'd find someone who sees me like you do. You've changed everything."

I look up at this sweet, gentle man. "I was so lost when I came here. I knew what I wanted to do with my life. I just didn't know how. I was running away, even though I didn't realize it at the time. Now I can do whatever I want, on my terms, and none of that was possible without you. You let me be me, you encouraged me to play my guitar and take photos and make friends. That person, the real Caitlyn, is someone I haven't seen for a while and I'm all the better for finding her again."

We fall silent, watch the sun start to sink into the sea. "I've never felt so much joy as I have since you came into my life. You're beautiful, inside and out. You make me laugh, you love my friends and my family *and* you accept that most of them are terrible people. You're not scared of anything, not even delivering a baby in a car," says Hank.

"I still can't believe I did that. And you are so wrong. I am scared of everything. I couldn't even get up the courage to tell you who I really was."

He holds on to me so tightly, his arms wrapping around me as if he is never going to let go. "The pain when I thought you were gone was unbearable. The idea of never being able to hold you in my arms again." He shivers. "It was devastating."

I look down at the pebbles and run my hand through them. Running away never solves anything, and yet Hank and I seem to be experts at it. "I'll never leave you again, no matter how hard it gets, no matter what we face. I promise we'll always try to work it out."

He picks up a pebble from the beach, pulls out a pen from his pocket and writes *Marry the Princess* on it, then throws it in to the sea.

"One day, when you're ready, maybe one year, ten years from now — who knows, maybe even tomorrow — I'm going to marry you, princess. I will always be here to keep you safe, I will always hold your hand, I will fight for you and I will always be on your side."

No woman in the world is as loved as I am, right here on this beach right now. I adore him so completely, utterly, without fear. I trust him and now he knows he can trust me.

We look out at the sun as the final rays disappear behind the horizon. The sun setting on the past.

A new adventure awaits, and it isn't going to be an easy one, we've got quite a few hurdles to get over, but we've got this far and I think we've proven we can face whatever comes our way.

"I love you, cowboy." He laughs. I haven't used that in a while.

He kisses the top of my head and pulls me closer "I love you, too, princess."

Want to see more from this author? Here's a taster for you to enjoy!

Mended Hearts: Liberating Jane
Katherine E Hunt

Excerpt

My hands were shaking. "I'm sorry." I was talking to the guy splayed out in front of me, but more importantly to my dead husband, whose ghost was probably floating around the room in bemusement right now.

I could almost hear the lighthearted derision in his voice as he berated me. *'I tell you to move on after I'm gone and you find some guy off Tinder?'* I wanted to tell him that getting over him was fucking impossible, that no man could ever fill his shoes, but you see, that's the problem with dead people—they're never around when you need to talk.

"Do you want to stop?" asked the very horny, very down-to-fuck, very not dead man in my bed.

"No. Please, I do want this." I did. I really, truly wanted this guy to fuck me senseless. It was just, well, awkward. This bed hadn't seen a man since David died and frankly it was weirding me out a little. I needed to stop messing about and get on with it. Get back on the bike or the horse, or in this case the huge dick.

I unbuttoned his shirt and pulled it open, scraping my nails across his chest, just enough to make him wince. Beverly's advice was perfect—getting your nails done for a date was a solid plan. I felt a lot less like a soccer mom and more like a sexy little minx. The buttons on his jeans popped open with ease, releasing him. I hadn't needed to take them off to see what I was dealing with—the bulge in his pants left nothing to the imagination—but holy cocksuckers, people, I was not disappointed with the beast I'd freed.

"Like what you see, huh?" he said, waving it in my face. I bent down to inspect it further. Straight as a die. As impeccably groomed as the rest of his body. I gave it a lick, just a tiny taste. *Hmmm. Okay.* I popped my mouth on, just to see. It fitted perfectly. A match made in heaven. His hands settled onto my head, gripping the roots of my hair, but the glare I threw him sent them scurrying away.

My terms—that was what we had agreed on. If we did it, we did it my way or not at all. I lifted my head. "You got protection?"

"Do I need it? I mean, aren't you on the pill or something?"

"What? I'm a fucking widow."

"You're right, sorry. I'm just used to, you know, younger women—they're always up for a bit of bareback."

"Jesus Christ." He smiled and winked at me. *Pathetic.* I took a deep breath and thought of the orgasms.

You can do this, Jane—just one quick fuck and you never have to see him again.

He handed me a condom. I slowly ripped it open with my teeth and slid it down on to his dick. It had been a while, but I still had it. Next thing to be sliding down that dick would be me and I couldn't wait any longer. It had been eight endless months since my husband had dearly departed this earth and, damn it, a woman has needs.

I climbed up his body and slid right down onto him. No need for foreplay — I'd practically come in my pants when he kissed me outside the restaurant.

Maybe I was seventeen and virginal once again. Or maybe he just had a big dick. Whatever the reason, I was tightly wrapped around him and it was amazing.

This wasn't such a bad idea after all.

I rode up and down on him just long enough to tire the muscles in my legs — about thirty seconds, to be honest, I hadn't exactly been hitting the gym lately — then rolled us over, pulling his hand onto my clit as we went.

"Make me come," I cried and prepared to be nailed into oblivion but he jerked and squealed a little, then flopped down onto me.

"Fuck, that was awesome."

"But..." *But my orgasm, you dickwad.*

"I think, no, I know it. I love you, Jane." Then, no word of a lie, he started to cry. I peeled him off me and mumbled something about needing a shower. *Shit.* He was in my house. How was I going to get him to leave? I thanked Madonna, the patron saint of sexual liberation, for having had the foresight to sell my house a few days before this disaster of a date. I'd soon be moving up the country to Massachusetts, as far away from this idiot as the moving truck could take me.

I headed downstairs, served myself a large bourbon, neat, and switched on my laptop. I clicked on my social media page, entered my password and started to type, 'Fuck it ladies, you are never going to believe what just happened.'

* * * *

It hadn't even been an hour, probably more like forty-five minutes before the casseroles started arriving. I'd read about it in the welcome pack that Beverly had been kind enough to email me, but the sheer amplitude of the visitors to my door was overwhelming to say the least.

This time it was three impeccably coiffed women in their early thirties who were hovering on my doorstep with a huge basket of carbs. The gentle warmth of the Cape Cod summer, far from the sweltering Florida heat I'd come from, relieved me of any obligation to invite them in.

"Hi, I'm Sally, this is Kendra and Barb. We were put in charge of desserts, so I made you some of my famous muffins."

"Thank you." I did what I thought probably looked like a smile. I'd taken an Ambien about half an hour ago, in the hope of getting in an afternoon nap before I needed to start unpacking, but clearly life had other plans. I could be naked in front of them right now and have no idea.

I should've invited them in—that would've been the polite thing to do—but the couch was still wrapped from the move. I didn't even know where my dining room chairs were and, quite frankly, I just couldn't give a shit about being polite on moving day. "I know what you're thinking, but don't you dare invite us in, we know exactly what it's like to move here alone. Trust me, you're going to need a good couple of days to get yourself sorted." *Thank you for small mercies.* I honestly couldn't cope with chitchat at the moment. Sleep had evaded me for, well, months and I'd rather poke my eyes out with sticks than make nice with strangers.

David had always been the one who had answered the door, dealt with people. I was more than happy to be the strong, silent woman behind the man. Until there was no man. And I was no longer strong. He'd been in my life since we were seventeen. Young love and an unexpected pregnancy had thrown us in the deep end, but I hadn't regretted it for a second, not even when his ailing body had failed him and I'd given up everything to spend the last year of his life nursing him twenty-four hours a day.

"We're having a little ladies' night on Saturday. Now, I know you're new and you don't know anybody yet, but you just have to come. Barb here is making margaritas and Beverly is setting us up a projector in the backyard. Romcoms and cocktails, it'll be a blast. Promise me you'll come."

"Oh well, I don't really…"

"Just give it a try." Kendra's voice was quieter and more restrained than Sally's. She gave me a smile that said 'I hate it too, but we have to do this kind of thing' and I knew exactly what she meant. For the last nine months, the whole world had been telling me I needed to go out, socialize, meet new people. That was how I'd ended up here in the first place. A widow's group on social media. When it came to selling the house, one of the girls had suggested Winchester Drive, and here I was. A gated community in a respectable part of the state. House prices were high, but this place was special. Over half of the homeowners were widows. *Cougar Town*, my son had called it when I'd announced my move.

"I would love to, thank you, ladies, that sounds really nice."

I closed the door and plonked down on the stairs. When I'd told the group that I was looking at a house on Winchester Drive I must have gotten over thirty new friend requests, plus an invitation to a more private group called the Winchester Widows.

They'd convinced me to stay more than anything else. No pressure to find a new husband. No shame in being a miserable bitch in public. *Wear black, they'd said, or hot pink or whatever the fuck you want. Weep loudly, party hard, drink a little too much or not at all. The WWs accepted your grief however the hell you wanted to do it and they didn't judge you an ounce.*

Plus, I thought as I bit into Sally's muffins, they made damn good desserts. *That, my friend, is exactly what the doctor ordered.*

Home of Erotic Romance

Sign up for our newsletter and find out about all our romance book releases, eBook sales and promotions, sneak peeks and FREE romance books!

About the Author

Katherine E Hunt ran off with a Frenchman twenty years ago. She now lives on a French mountain with three children and two dogs. When she isn't writing contemporary romance she can be found huddled up in front of a roaring fire, with a glass of Chardonnay in one hand and a book in the other.

Katherine loves to hear from readers. You can find her contact information, website details and author profile page at https://www.totallybound.com

www.ingramcontent.com/pod-product-compliance
Lightning Source LLC
Chambersburg PA
CBHW05073118O626
46814CB00002B/706